THE TRASH MAN

JUSTICE FOR ALL

By Norm Meech

Tellwell Talent
www.tellwell.ca

ISBN
978-0-2288-1619-5 (Hardcover)
978-0-2288-1618-8 (Paperback)
978-0-2288-1620-1 (eBook)

DEDICATION

To my wife Monica, my son Hunter and my daughter Haleigh:
You are my inspiration and the best part of my life.

TABLE OF CONTENTS

SUMMARY

After being a policeman for over 30 years, Alex McNeil retires and, to supplement his pension, starts driving a garbage truck in one of the roughest areas of Bisson City, a small, tough little city in southern Ontario.

Alex resides just outside of Bisson City in a quiet suburban area. He expects his new career to be relatively stress-free, and, at 60 years of age, thinks he has left the policing world behind him. However, his old-school, hard-nose, stubborn homicide cop reputation follows him into retirement—and when a prostitute Alex knows is sexually assaulted and brutally murdered, he allows himself to be dragged into the murder investigation.

Along the way, he renews his friendship with his former partner, Inspector Stephanie Foster, who is the lead investigator on the case—which Alex soon finds out is a *string* of prostitute murders.

As Alex and Stephanie race against time to solve the murders and bring a serial killer to justice, Alex also struggles with his relationship with Stephanie—a woman for whom he feels more than mere friendship …

CHAPTER I

I put my lunch and water bottle into my pickup and left for work. *It's 9:45 p.m. at night and here I go again,* I think, as I cruise down the highway to Bisson City. *If the traffic moves well, it's should only be about 45 minutes until I get to work.*

After working for over 30 years in policing, I still can't believe I'm working the night shift (from 11:00 p.m. to 7:00 a.m., four times a week) as a garbage man. It's not something I ever expected to be doing, but I don't mind it and it keeps me busy. It's pretty easy work. I drive a trash truck and I pick up and empty container bins in the darkness of Bisson City, in southern Ontario, where I enjoyed working as a police officer for 30 years. But 30 years was long enough. Most cops retire long before that, and I can understand why.

When I was working as a cop I grew accustomed to a certain type of lifestyle, but being a cop isn't exactly the way to get rich, so, when I retired, I decided to supplement my pension by working part-time. Coincidentally, after a couple of months of idling about, I met an old buddy—Allan Featherstone, another retired cop—for lunch one day. Unlike me, Allan was doing okay with money. He'd received an inheritance from his father, started a container bin business and had quickly snapped up a city waste contract. Allan's business, Featherstone Container Bins, had about 300 bins across the city and employed six trucks and 14 drivers, of which I am one.

When we got to talking, Allan told me he couldn't find anyone

1

to work the night shift in the core of Bisson City, so he offered me the job. I thought ... *what the hell, it sounds like a good gig ...* and took it. Mostly I like it, but sometimes it's a bit dodgy. There are a lot of isolated and rough areas in the city, and of course this is where garbage and cardboard bins are generally located. Some of these locations are in laneways behind businesses, and they're frequented by drug addicts, drunks, transients and hookers. Not really a problem for me; as a former cop, I'm accustomed to such people. I don't mind them and I know how to deal with them. And taking the night shift worked in my favour—Allan pays me a bit more than the other drivers to work that shift.

The job itself is simple. Most of the time, I don't even have to get out of the truck; I just line up the hydraulic lift forks with the container slots, lift the container and dump the contents in the back. When the truck is full, depending on whether I'm hauling cardboard or garbage, I either drive east to the transfer station to dump the cardboard, or take the garbage to the west end dump. Then I get a couple of signatures on the invoices and leave the dump slips on a clip board for Allan. That's it. It's easy and safe as long as I remain aware of my surrounding ... and it helps that I don't have to get out of the truck that often. Plus I get to drive and work at my own pace.

Some nights I get certain sections of my run done a little more quickly than others and that gives me some downtime. When that happens, I have a couple of different places I like to stop at for a coffee or a bite to eat. Like in all downtowns of all big cities, Bisson City has its share of pretty rough coffee shops, and when you frequent them as late as I do you have to watch your back. I learned a long time ago to be aware of my surroundings at all times. That having been said, I also believe that when it comes to some of the crazy night people I meet, you can't always judge a book by its cover. Not everyone is dangerous. We all have different stories and life paths and until someone shows me they're really not worth my time, I treat everyone with respect.

After midnight the downtown core comes alive in a way that it doesn't during the day. That's when the night people come out—transients, drug addicts and prostitutes looking for action, drugs, company or shelter. Every one of them has his or her own story about how they ended up on the street and homeless; in or out of rehab; scared and alone. Some of them have been abused; some wound up with drug habits they couldn't kick; some suffer from mental health issues and just fell through the cracks of society … all have had some type of life-altering experience.

During my downtown travels, I often see Old Joe, a homeless fellow who seems to have been old since the day he was born. Old Joe wanders around all over the city, pushing his shopping cart in front of him. The cart holds about 50 plastic bags, filled with his worldly possessions. Bearded and scruffy, few people notice him, and most cross the street to avoid him. I'd seen him a lot when I was a cop, but I never really talked to him until I started driving the garbage truck, which was about four months ago. One night I went down a laneway off Jarvis and Devine Streets to unload a bin full of cardboard. I happened to notice Old Joe's plastic bag-adorned shopping cart next to a bin. I got out of the truck with Bertha, my baseball bat, banged on the bin, and Joe popped his head out, surprising me. He had been curled up in the cardboard, trying to keep warm. I thought, *damn, he doesn't know how lucky he is that I saw his cart!* If I'd dumped the bin into the truck without checking, I'd have never heard him scream over the noise of compactor. I made a mental note to always look for signs of life around the bins before dumping them.

That night, Joe and I spoke for about 15 minutes and then he went on his way. A few weeks later, however, I ran into him at the Jarvis Street coffee shop and bought him a coffee. I'm not going to lie; he was dirty and smelly, which repulsed me a bit; but after talking to him for a while I got over it. He kind of warmed up to me, and before long he told me about his past and it really put a face on what some people have to live through. He said he used to be a successful bank manager and had once been married with two children. He didn't really like his job—it was very stressful—but it allowed him to financially support his family. Then his eyes teared up as he told me about a day that changed his life forever. He was hard at work when he got an afternoon phone call from the police, telling him to go the emergency room at the Bisson Hospital. "Your wife and children have been seriously injured in a car accident," a woman's voice told him

When Joe arrived at the hospital, he was immediately escorted into a private room. He didn't understand why and kept asking how his wife and kids were.

"When no one gave me a firm answer, that's when I realized something was really wrong," he said, still clearly upset at the thought of that moment. He stared down into his coffee. "The doctor said emergency staff did everything they could to save them, but it was a high-speed collision caused by a drunk driver, and they couldn't be saved."

And that is how, in one terrible afternoon he lost his entire family … and the life he thought was secure and stable changed forever. *There but for the grace of God go I,* I thought. Joe and all his plastic bags full of stuff suddenly made a lot more sense. That junk was all he had left to care for.

Joe is just one of the characters that live downtown and hang around those late-night greasy spoons. There are a host of others. I have met and spoken to hookers, strippers, alcoholics, drug addicts and runaways, among others. There are very few 'normals' frequenting these establishments, especially at this time of night. Instead, you meet the marginalized, with their sad and tragic stories. In my cop uniform, when I looked at these people, I saw trouble. What I see now, in my smelly trash man overalls, is the humanity of these folks, because they talk to Alex the trash man in a way they would never talk to Alex the cop. They tell me their stories. Some of the hookers are single parents, or are trying to go to school, or are just trying to pay their rent. The strippers are the same. They do what they have to do to make money and survive, just like all of us. Then there are people with mental health issues, like Old Joe, or the ones with substance abuse issues. Some of them really want to get better and harbor dreams of reintegrating into society; others have just given up and want to die. That's always sad, and it makes me wonder which came first—the mental illness or the substance abuse? It's a chicken and egg question and the answer is different for everyone.

When I stop at the different coffee shops, most of the street people recognise me now. They know my truck and they know who I am. Some people call me Alex, or Alex the trash man, or simply—the trash man. I am a large man, six foot four and over 240 pounds, so in general I'm pretty noticeable, but something interesting I've realized since I took this garbage job is that, despite my size, it's only the street people who acknowledge me now. As a cop, I was always acknowledged. As a civilian in normal streetwear, I am always acknowledged. But as a garbage man, people are repulsed. Experiencing rejection in this way makes me feel connected to my new friends in a way not much else could.

I have not told any of my new acquaintances about my former profession. While I'm proud and lucky to have worked in law enforcement, I don't want any problems, so I decided it was best not to tell them. Once a cop, always a cop—I know that, and they do too. I also don't mention that I have a wife or children ... and I never tell anyone where I live.

Tonight is Sunday night, the first day of my four-night garbage shift. I work Sunday to Wednesday, starting at 11:00 p.m. and finishing at 6:45 a.m. Allan makes sure the day shift guys leave the truck clean and full of fuel and I have a key, so all I have to do is park my pickup, lock it, and then climb into the green, ten-ton tandem truck—with front end loader forks, a compacter in the back and a rear tilt lift to empty out the garbage—and go.

I usually start my shift with a coffee from Pete's coffee shop at Jarvis Street and Devine, followed by the 'cardboard route'.

Because cardboard doesn't mess up the back of the truck, it's picked up and dropped off at the recycling depot in the east end of Bisson City before I do the garbage run. When the cardboard is done, I have another coffee and then collect all the garbage, finishing my shift by emptying my load in the west end and cleaning out the truck. I don't rush the routes and I have lots of time for breaks. I'm usually in time to see Karen, my wife, off to work at around eight.

As usual, tonight I got in the big truck and drove down to Pete's. I pulled up and parked. People were milling about on the street and it was warm and muggy. I noticed the regular girls out on the corner trying to pick up some business. It's amazing the clothing they wear, a bit over-the-top, though I know that it's part of the business. Over time I've gotten to know some of their names, and I recognise most of the faces. They're generally young enough to be my daughter … and in some cases, my grand-daughter. They know me too, and now that they know I'm not interested in paying for sex, they joke with me and suggestively tease me instead of propositioning me. I give them the gears right back, throwing mild sexual innuendos their way. It makes them laugh. Some of the girls are very attractive, and I can't help but discreetly check them out. I'm old, but I'm not dead—or blind.

Most of the hookers called me 'the trash man'. I don't really care what they call me, or what they think of me, for that matter. I think of them as slightly off-kilter friends. I like to verbally joust with them and I always finish the conversation by telling them to be careful when they're choosing their clients. Truthfully, I worry about them. Hooking is a pretty high-risk job. In the past year, four hookers have been murdered in the downtown area, sexually assaulted first, if the news is to be believed. Two bodies were found in the water adjacent to the harbour warehouse, and two in laneways—laneways I could have driven down in my garbage truck. It makes me cold to think of it. *The killer dumps their bodies like garbage*, I thought, *leaving them in public view.*

In particular, I was sad about the third girl who was killed, because I knew her, at least a little. Sally Armstrong was just 20 years old and she was killed shortly after I started this job, when I was first getting to know her and a few of the other night people. She was a good-looking girl, black with really pretty, dark eyes and a sweet smile. She was one of the first of the hookers to talk to me and tell me her story. She was sexually and physically abused by a neighbor when she was a kid and when she was about 14 years old she ran away from home and got addicted to crack cocaine. To support her habit, what else could she do but turn tricks? It was all she knew—that her body had value to men. It became a vicious cycle; sexual abuse got her into her mess and sexual abuse was all she could do to keep her head above water. Every time I saw her, she told me she was trying to clean herself up and every time I saw her she was still out of it. The drugs allowed her to escape her nightmares. It's tough to escape that life without the proper support.

I still remember the first time I met her. I had to go down a laneway off Vermont Drive to pick up a bin and, since I was new on the job, I was unaware that this was 'Sally's laneway' and that when she picked up tricks she would often service them next to a particular bin. As I got close to 'her' bin, I wasn't sure what I was seeing at first, just a dark shape moving rhythmically in the night, but as the truck's headlights shone down the laneway I realized it was two bodies, a man and a beautiful girl. He looked sheepish and dismayed as my headlights shone on them, but she just yelled, "Hey trash man, can you wait a few minutes?"

A few weeks later, as fate would have it, I saw her in the same laneway with a local guy hustler named Larry Mann. I recognized her right away from the mop of curly black hair and her shapely figure—I can always recognize a girl's curves. But as I pulled the big truck into the lane, I realized things didn't look good. Larry was yelling at Sally and then he hauled off and hit her. I immediately figured out that he must be her pimp. I stopped the truck and got out, with Bertha (my baseball bat) in my right hand.

Larry looked at me belligerently. "What do you want, trash man?" he snarled.

I kept a good grip on Bertha as I told him, "You stop beating on her."

"This is none of your business," he retorted, his eyes narrowing.

I knew he was probably carrying a gun and that I really shouldn't get him going, so I said to him, "Listen, can't we work something out here?" He looked at me like I was crazy, and I continued, "She's not going to earn you any money all beat up. What would it take for you to stop beating her?"

"Bitch still owes me a hundred dollars," Larry said.

I realized I had around a hundred bucks in my pocket, so I took the money out and said, "Here's the money, take it."

Larry took the money and counted it. He seemed satisfied. He nodded at Sally, as if to say, 'you're off the hook,' and turned to go. As he was walking away, he turned and said, "Trash man, you better mind your own business. Next time, you may not be as lucky."

If I had still been a cop, I would have cuffed that guy so fast … but there was nothing I could do. I just let him walk away and stared holes into his back.

I looked at Sally. She had a bloody lip, a blackened eye and was holding her side. I wondered if he'd punched her in the kidney. I was worried for her. I touched her arm and said, "Come on, let's go … get in the truck." She decided to trust me and did as I said.

I took her to a nearby restaurant and she went to the washroom to clean herself up. I had some spare money in my coat, so I bought her something to eat. We sat and talked for about 30 minutes. She asked me, "Do you always carry that much money in your wallet?"

I do, but I thought it best she didn't know that, so I lied and said, "I was going to put some gas in the truck at the end of my shift."

"We could have sex for the hundred bucks I owe you," she suggested.

"Thanks, but no thanks," I told her with a careful smile. I didn't want to offend her; sex was all she had to trade, after all. I added, "Don't worry about the money. I'm good. I just want you to stay safe out there."

"What are you, a cop or something?" she kidded. I just smiled. There was no way I was going to tell her she'd almost nailed it. Then she said, "You're the first person who's done something like this for me without wanting something in return." And that's when she told me about her life growing up. She said the neighbor abused her and her parents did not believe what she was going through. In fact, they kept having the man over for drinking parties and when they passed out he would sneak into her room and force himself on her, starting when she was just a little girl. She tried to tell them again and her mother called her a whore and a liar. Finally, Sally left.

"I wish I could get out of hooking," she said wistfully. "I always wanted to be a hairdresser. But it costs a lot to go to school and you need to have stable life." She sighed. "I don't know any other way to make money." I never said anything. I just listened. When she left, she said, "Thanks, Alex." I smiled with pleasure. The other girls always called me 'the trash man'.

When Sally was murdered, it really took the wind out of my sails. She was a gorgeous kid and a sweet soul. She could have been my daughter. Certainly she was *someone's* daughter, even if those parents hadn't treated her in the way good parents should. For me, Sally's death made what was slowly becoming a hot topic in the media very personal. Before her death, I just did my trash man job and tried to avoid getting interested in what was going on, as it brought out the cop in me and made me miss my old life. But after the murder, I started researching every bit of media coverage on what was becoming known as 'the prostitute murders', trying to read between the lines with my special police mindset. I knew the police always held their trump cards close to their chest and didn't release everything they knew to the media so they could have one special fact that only the killer would know. And I wanted to know what that was.

CHAPTER 2

Of the 30 years I spent as a cop, over 12 were spent working homicide. I still remember every detail of every murder investigated; each and every one of the victims; their families; and, the inevitable brutality of the crimes. Murder is rarely gentle. It still bothers me that I couldn't solve all the cases I was involved with. But you can't win 'em all, as they say.

Given my background, I knew the Bisson City Homicide Unit was probably under a lot of pressure to make an arrest and that they would also have a large team of investigators assigned to the four murders. Although the media had released a lot of information in their stories, I was sure the police had more—but they weren't saying.

In every murder investigation, there is what is called 'hold back' evidence that only the case manager or lead investigator is aware of. Hold back evidence is specific evidence related to the killer. It could be the killer's modus operandi (M.O.), physical evidence (such as DNA), or any evidence only the killer would be aware of or linked to. I was hoping that by reading the newspapers, I might get an idea of what that was by reading between the lines with my cop senses.

As I reviewed information online, I found out that, although the victims were sexually assaulted, police had not released information about what had actually caused their deaths. All I could find out was that witnesses at the crime scenes (generally those who'd discovered the bodies) said none of them looked beat up. This made me wonder, *were they strangled or suffocated?* The police would know, as they would have results of the post mortem exams and a pathologist would have determined the cause of death. However I suspected that the coroner probably hadn't released that information to the victim's family yet. Since all the deaths were homicides, the police were probably only releasing basic information to protect the integrity of the investigation.

These thoughts went around and around in my head as I continued to drive my garbage route and soon—despite telling myself to let it go, that I was no longer a cop—all the specific elements necessary to conduct a murder investigation were back full-force in my brain. I had dealt with multiple murder victims in the past, but never a string of murders. Of course I was intrigued. There was no doubt in my mind that the police had a serial killer on their hands. What I didn't know was if the murders were linked through evidence.

I knew investigators probably had a ton of information to sort through. They would be processing crime scene evidence, interviewing witnesses, reviewing victims' backgrounds, digging up profiles on sex offenders, and following up on all tips. They would be looking for any forensic evidence that might link the cases together: DNA, semen, salvia, hair … *anything*. I trusted that Sally's killer would soon be found by the men and women in blue who I knew so well, and at first there was a flurry of activity downtown, including extra patrol cars driving around keeping an eye on the working girls. However, I didn't observe police investigators out actually *talking* to the prostitutes, and soon that started to die down. Next, even the media lost interest. With the police not releasing much juicy information, beyond putting two and two together and hinting at the presence of a serial killer, they had nothing. Soon, a month was gone and the killer was still out there. I wondered, *if the victims weren't prostitutes, would there be more public pressure to catch the bad guys?* I was willing to bet four murders in the rich part of the city would have got a lot more interest and resources.

By now, I was fully in cop mode and I couldn't believe how fast my nights were going by as I drove around thinking about the murders, my mind going a hundred miles a minute. I thought I'd left my cop persona behind me when I retired, but clearly I had not. I just couldn't get over Sally's death. It really got to me that nothing was being done. She was a sweet kid and didn't deserve to die in an alley like that. I wanted to do something to help, but then I thought, *I'm an old, retired cop. I'm out of touch with investigative methods and technology. I don't have access to any police information. I'm only guessing as to what's going on with these murder investigations.*

But I couldn't stop thinking about it.

I don't really remember driving up the highway and arriving home. Karen was about to leave to go to work. "How was your night?" she asked.

"Okay," I said. Then I kissed her goodbye and I told her I would call her later.

"Get some sleep," she said as she left.

I sat on the living room couch and looked around my house. I wasn't ready to go to bed yet. *The house is so quiet,* I thought. My son, Jamie, moved out about six years ago to go to university, and then was hired by the city of Kingston as a mental health care worker. He's got his own life now, though still comes home for holidays and family get-togethers when he can. My daughter Chloe was attending university in London, Ontario. She was working on her degree in sports medicine, specializing in kinesiology and living just outside London with a couple of girlfriends.

They grow up so fast, I thought as I stared at the wall, feeling the emptiness of the house. It's sad at times to think how it all went by in a blur. But I'm lucky, I guess. They are good kids and have matured into good, self-sufficient adults and I'm very proud of both of them.

The other member of the family, Kobe, died just a few years ago. Kobe was our yellow lab. He lived to the age of eight, which is pretty good for a big dog. He died from cancer of the nose. It broke my heart. He was my buddy and when he died, it felt like I lost a kid. In some ways he was more of a kid to me than my actual kids. They grew up and became people in the world, but he was always my loyal pup. He loved me and needed me no matter what. I miss him terribly. I still speak to him when I'm alone in the house.

I smiled as I thought about him. "I miss you, boy," I said softly to the urn with his ashes in it that sits on the mantle over the fireplace, watching over us.

Kobe was a good dog. He was a loving family pet and my biggest fan. No matter what shift I worked, or what time I came home, Kobe was always awake and happy to see me, his tail wagging as he pranced around in greeting like a puppy. When he got a little older, like all of us, he slowed down, and then when I got home instead of doing the greeting dance he'd raise his head from where he lay on the couch and wag his tail in acknowledgement. He was too tired to get up; now I had to go over to him to scratch his ears.

Most days Kobe got walked three times, in the morning and at night by Karen and me, and when we were at work, by a dog walker. On the weekends Karen and I took him for long jaunts, sometimes as long as five miles, through the nearby ravine, our favorite place. Walking with Kobe kept us in shape. I miss him still.

After a few more minutes of thinking about Kobe, I realized I was finally tired enough to go to bed. I slept for about five hours, though I got up twice to piss. The phone rang once and one of the neighbours cut his grass … and then it was time to get up. I don't think anyone really understands how difficult it is to sleep through the day unless they have worked night shifts themselves.

I wasn't at all refreshed when I got up to wash my face—and I couldn't stop thinking about the murders. I made myself a coffee and then got on the Internet. I needed to satisfy my curiosity, at least that's what I told myself. Soon, however, I'd built an electronic filing system and started compiling information. I called it, *Life*. I didn't want to call it *Murder Investigation* in case Karen got on the computer and got worried about what I was up to. She wants me to take it easy and enjoy my semi-retirement. She's always said the cop life was going to kill me.

As I poke around on the web, I think, *it's amazing how much technology has developed in the last 25 years.* It has certainly changed the policing world. You can obtain huge amounts of information from the Internet; sometimes criminals brag about their crimes on Facebook, and you can just cut, paste and arrest. Confession online. Guys *that* stupid deserve to be busted.

There is also easy access to cross-department databases. You can find or move data with a push of a key. *The keys I used when I was a new, young police officer were on a typewriter,* I think wryly. But I like the new way of doing things. In the old days, we had boxes full of investigative paperwork and, depending on the filing system, it could take days to find various documents. Today it takes mere minutes.

For the next two weeks I downloaded as much information as I could find on the four murders. I read all the different Bisson newspaper stories; I visit the Bisson police homicide website for information; and, some days, I spent all day researching the serial killers in general, like Paul Bernando and Karla Homolka, famous Canadian killers. *What makes them tick? How does it apply to what has happened here in Bisson City?*

I was careful not to spend much time on the computer when Karen was home. I knew she would be pissed off if she knew I'd put my cop hat back on. We've been married 30 years and no one was happier to see me retire than her. She knows the horrendous hours I used to work and the stress I used to shoulder. I never got enough sleep, had poor eating habits and sometimes drank too much. I gained and lost unhealthy amounts of weight. I'm sure police work contributed to an ongoing heart problem over the years—that and the fact that heart problems run in my family. But despite her worrying and despite the stress, I am still proud to have been a cop, especially a homicide cop. I firmly believe the greatest honour and responsibility a police officer can ever have is to be responsible for investigating someone's death. *We all matter and none of us are disposable*—that is the credo a good homicide investigator brings with him or her to every case, me included.

So, even though I felt like I was cheating on Karen, I created five sub-folders in my filing system, one for each murder and one full of general information on serial killers, or whatever I found that I thought might be useful. It's basic information, but it's a good start.

BRENDA SMITH: The first victim's body was found, partially clothed, on Thursday, June 12, at 8:00 a.m., floating in the water at the base of Cherry Street. She was 21 years old, Caucasian, slender, and had light-brown hair. The local newspapers said she was a prostitute who frequented the intersection of Dundas Street and Vermont Drive. Witnesses said she'd last been seen around 2:00 a.m. on the morning of her death, approaching vehicles that stopped just east of Vermont Drive. The coroner's report indicated she had probably died within six hours of being found and that she had only been in the water for a brief period of time. A police media release a few weeks after the murder asked for the public's assistance in locating a blue or green minivan, operated by a male, 40 to 60 years of age.

I looked at Brenda's picture which had been posted online in one of the articles I found, but she didn't look familiar.

LINDA TURNER: The second murder happened in the early hours of Monday, September 2, four months later. Linda Turner's partially-clad body was found in a laneway, off a side-street running between Queen Street and Adelaide Street East by a businesswoman who was taking a shortcut through the laneway on her lunch break. This woman confirmed to reporters that, except for the lack of clothing, Linda had no visible external injuries. Police media releases indicated she was 20 years old, slender, and had short, blonde hair. Linda had apparently just moved to Ontario from Alberta a few months prior to her death.

Although I'd never met Linda, when I saw her picture, she looked familiar. I thought she might be one of the girls who'd worked the corner of Jarvis and Devine once in a while. Some girls only worked the last few days of the week because there was a lot more business around payday. I checked my work schedule. I had been working for Allen just a couple of weeks the night Linda disappeared, and I was working that night but had not been down the laneway where she was found.

SALLY ARMSTRONG: The third murder victim was Sally. Her body was found in the laneway adjacent to the one where I occasionally saw her in with her customers. Sally was black, 20 years old and, at the time of her death, she'd dyed her shoulder-length, kinked hair blonde. She was found Wednesday, December 12, at 10:00 a.m. by a parking control officer who had been out tagging cars in the fire route that morning. I checked my schedule again; I worked that night, but I have no memory of seeing Sally. I didn't even know she'd dyed her hair.

I still remember the shock of finding out about her murder on the evening news. Sally's picture flashed up on the TV screen as the reporter announced that she was the third prostitute killed in less than a year. The news story showed pictures of the crime scene. I recognised the laneway immediately. And then I recognized the detective in charge of Bisson Police Service's newly formed homicide task force—Detective Inspector Stephanie Foster.

I'd known Stephanie well at one time. We'd met about 12 years before, at a police homicide conference. She was a sergeant at the time and had just been transferred into the homicide unit. She was a good-looking, smart investigator who'd started developing her homicide knowledge and skills with the goal of moving up the food chain to solve the big murders. She was ambitious and bright, and I liked her right away.

Shortly after that, we wound up working together, both of us seconded to a joint forces, multi-jurisdictional investigation into the abduction and murder of an eight-year-old boy. We spent over a year working side-by-side as partners and we got to be pretty good friends. It was a very tough and emotional investigation and you don't get through something like that without forming some deep bonds with the people who share the experience with you. I like to think there was a bit of personal feeling on both sides too. I'm not going to lie, there was sure some on mine. But I was about 50 at the time and she was around 30—I was old enough to be her father, which really bugged me. Toss in the fact that were both married, and the answer to anything personal was … *forget it*. But I never forgot *her*. She was quite a woman. She had brains, looks, personality and a great ass to boot.

After the investigation was over (yes, we caught the bastard) we continued to talk a bit on the phone, but when the trial ended, we stopped. I did a quick count and realized it had probably been about ten years since I'd spoken to her. But I'd always known where she was. Stephanie is one of the rare officers who has spent almost their entire career in one unit. In the time since I'd last seen her, she'd only left the homicide unit for two six-month periods, each time after a promotion. They wanted her there and it was where she belonged. I was sure she had become a very knowledgeable investigator.

JOAN WHITE: The fourth victim was 19-year-old Joan White. Joan's body was found only a week ago, around 7:00 a.m., January 15. Some fishermen found her body on the rocky shoreline near where the river empties into the lake. The news suggested she was dumped in the river and the current carried her body downstream. Joan's profile was similar to that of the other victims; a prostitute, around 20, slim build, blondish hair. It was reported that she was found naked. I guessed that the river current probably caused her clothing to fall off. I also guessed she probably had trauma to her body from hitting rocks and such while floating downstream. River critters probably also had a nibble on her. That's nature for you.

I knew the priority for the investigative team would be to determine where she went into the river, known as the 'dump location'. Using statistics on wind speed and river flow, they would determine that, and then they would look for physical evidence at the river's edge to support the theory of dump and float.

There was no doubt a serial killer saw at work. My seasoned cop reasoning had already determined that the builds of the dead women were the same and all but Sally were Caucasian and blond. She was the one who didn't fit, but I wondered, *if she doesn't fit, maybe there are others who don't. Maybe the scope of the investigation should be increased.* I started looking online for similar deaths, to see if there was anything the police and newspapers were potentially not seeing. It wasn't long before I came across a story about a transvestite named Bobbi (Robert) Thompson, who'd been murdered on April 29. Bobbi was a 20-year-old male transvestite who had been working as a prostitute off Jarvis Street. When he was found murdered, he was dressed in female clothing and wearing a long blonde hair wig. Like Sally and Linda, Bobbi was found in a laneway off Vermont Drive. But unlike any of the other dead prostitutes, witnesses described extreme trauma to his body. This murder was covered by the media as a homosexual hate crime. It remained unsolved.

A bit more research on my part revealed a follow-up story a few days later, in which a late-night dog-walker said that, the night before Bobbi's body was found, she had seen an older blue, or possibly green, van in that very laneway. She'd watched two medium- to heavily-built Caucasian males get in it and drive away. At the time, she'd thought it strange to see a van in the laneway and wondered if they were rooting through peoples' garbage or picking bottles or something. It was night so she didn't see their faces or get their hair colour.

This new information gave me pause. While prostitution in general is a high-risk profession, in my mind transvestites or transgender prostitutes are most vulnerable. If a john is looking for a tranny for a fetish kick or something, that's great. But if he finds out *after* the fact that it's a *guy* sucking his dick, things can get a bit hairy. Some people really take offense to that and, depending on the customer's personality, there can be some dangerous reactions. The extreme trauma to Thompson's body suggested that hate had fuelled the violence. I wondered if that was why. And then I started a new file called *Bobbi Thompson*.

CHAPTER 3

It was another Sunday night—the start of a work week for me. Although I'd had a quick nap before work, I was tired. Night shifts are strange. Even when I was a cop, it never seemed natural or normal to work through the night when everybody else is sleeping. Besides feeling tired and a bit disoriented, I also couldn't stop my mind from churning and wondering about the murders. I kept asking myself, *why the hell do I care? I'm not a cop. I now drive a garbage truck. Why am I wasting all my spare time researching these murders?*

But deep inside, I knew why I cared. I became a police officer because I wanted to help people and because I believed in a system of law and order, and in justice for all. And even though I was no longer a cop, I still believed in those things. The system is not perfect, but it's the only system we have. As corny as it sounds, I feel strongly that, 'if you do the crime, you should do the time.' That killer had to be caught and punished.

I pulled up to Pete's and went inside and had a coffee. A couple of the girls on the corner razzed me as usual. I smiled and told them they looked beautiful. They liked that. When my coffee was done, I took a smaller one to go and then I hopped in my truck. It wasn't spring yet, but I opened the truck window and drove around with the cold air blowing in my face. The breeze helped keep me awake and alert.

As per my usual, first I did the cardboard run and then when

I was done, I went back to the city core to start the garbage route. The garbage run is always more interesting. Where there is stinky, smelly garbage there are also huge rats. Downtown, the rats are used to people and they don't run away. They are so fat and slow that I could hit them with my baseball bat if I wanted to, but I don't. I let them be. They're doing their job, same as me. Nevertheless, I'm glad I don't have to get out of my truck much and get too friendly with them. I just line the truck's loading forks up with the slots on the bin, pick up the bin and dump it behind me. The only time I have to get out is if the bin is at an awkward angle and I have to push it into position.

The evening went smoothly until I pulled into a laneway on King Street, just east of Vermont Drive, to get the bin at the rear of the Hot Tomato Bistro. This particular laneway is about two and a half cars wide and it's tight for my truck, but I can just squeeze by the parked cars if I'm careful. It was 3:30 a.m. and I was almost ready for another coffee, but I wanted to pick this bin up first, so I started carefully maneuvering the truck down the lane. All of a sudden I saw ahead of me, over by the bin, a couple of people—probably drunks. *Shit*, I thought, *someone barfed or something over there. I'm definitely not getting out of the truck.* But as soon as my headlights hit the pair, instead of stumbling around, they got agitated, jumped into a van parked nearby, and sped off.

As they raced away, they hit a bunch of garbage cans and piled-up boxes. *Idiots*, I though. *What a fucking mess.* I decided I'd pick up the spilled cans after I'd emptied the dumpster, as they were blocking the laneway. I was kind of pissed about it, though.

I lined up the forks of the truck and started to lift the garbage bin, watching it through the front window of my truck as it rose. Then I saw something laying just behind the spot where the bin had sat moments before. It looked like a body. Instantly I went cold and my mind started clicking. I remembered the story I'd read where the dog-walker said she'd seen a van. *Damn*, I thought. *What're the odds?* Immediately, I jumped out of the truck, and ran over to the figure, already certain about what I would find. As I thought, it was a young woman, and she looked dead. She had a clear plastic bag over her head which I immediately ripped it off. I checked for a pulse; I wasn't sure, but there seemed to be a very faint one. I held her hand. "It's okay, sweetheart," I said to her. I continued to squeeze her fingers in mine as dialed 911 on my cell one-handed.

"Operator, I have found a woman in distress. I need police and an ambulance right away," I advised the operator. Then I told her where I was and what the condition of the victim was. Now I just had to wait.

I glanced around the scene as I continued to try to massage the young woman's wrist, trying to let her know someone was there and that someone cared. Her clothes were ripped open and her short dress rode high on her hips. She was not wearing any underwear, so out of respect I pulled her dress down a bit so she wouldn't be remembered like that by the first responders. I didn't want to mess with a crime scene, but really she needed *some* dignity.

It seemed like eternity but it really took only a few minutes for the police and ambulance to arrive. The paramedics told me she was still alive, but in rough shape. "You probably saved her life, sir," one of them told me.

A young uniformed officer told me not to move my truck and to wait for the detectives to show up. I did as he asked. As I sat on a nearby railing and watched the local law enforcement take control, I had no doubt that I'd seen the killers. Like it or not, I was now involved in the murder, even if I wasn't a cop anymore.

I tried to remember the vehicle so I could describe it to the investigators when they asked me. The lighting was poor and my truck's headlights only flashed on the two people for half a second so I didn't have much to offer them. And I only saw the rear of the van. But I knew from my years in law enforcement that it's often the smallest details that matter most. *I have to think. I have to remember what I saw.*

The officers had secured an interior and outer perimeter and I was just sitting there watching them when I heard a familiar voice, "Alex, is that you?"

I turned around and saw Stephanie and another officer walking toward me. She looked great. She was wearing a dark-blue business suit and a white, open-collared shirt. She looked so professional.

"Yes, it's me," I said, feeling surprisingly shy. I'm sure she knew I'd retired, but not that I'd picked up a gig as a trash man. However, if it surprised her, she didn't show it. Instead she hugged me as if it had only been days instead of years since we'd seen each other.

"You haven't changed a bit!" she said sincerely. She was either the world's best liar, or she meant it.

She introduced me to her partner, Corey Stinson. Corey shook my hand and asked, "So how do you know each other?"

"We were partners once," Stephanie told him. "We worked a homicide investigation together for about a year."

Corey looked surprised. I guess he couldn't reconcile the trash man outfit with a badge. I ignored him as I asked Stephanie, "How is the victim doing?

"Unfortunately she died in the ambulance on the way to the hospital," she informed me sadly. Then, "I hear you were first on the scene. That makes you a witness, Alex."

"I know," I told her.

"So tell me what you observed," she said as she got out her notebook.

I started at the top, how I'd noticed a couple of guys and thought they were drunks and how they'd fled when my lights hit them. I told her I saw the back of the van and later, when I lifted the bin, I discovered the girl. I made a point to tell her I'd moved her dress a bit and that it appeared to me at first glance that the girl was probably the victim of a sexual assault.

"You'll have to go to the police station and give a witness statement," she said.

"I know, no problem," I told her. "But I have to get the truck back to the yard soon for the day shift guys. Can you ask your people to speed it up a little?"

"Yeah, sure," she said. Then Stephanie told the forensics guys to process the truck first so it could be released in a few hours. I guessed that the laneway and the rest of the scene would probably take about 24 hours or more to process.

Stephanie and Corey gave me a ride to the police station. I hadn't been inside a police station for a few years. It was different entering one as a civilian witness instead of as a cop. It felt like I no longer belonged there, yet the intensity and excitement still stirred my soul.

There were a lot of reporters gathered around the station as we went inside. The word was out that another woman had been murdered, and it was only a matter of time until someone confirmed it was another prostitute. I was pretty sure she was, given the clothing she had been wearing, and the murder had happened in a laneway like two of the others.

When we got to the cop shop, there were a lot of officers running around, clearly trying to get a jump on this new murder. Stephanie asked Corey to get me a coffee. Then she asked me to sit down and wait while she went to update her bosses on the preliminary stages of the investigation.

I sat in the lobby and waited as asked. When Stephanie returned, she told me, "I'm not going to be the one to interview you. I have to avoid any possible conflict, since we worked together. But your eye witness statement is important, so Corey will interview you."

In a few moments, Corey showed up and escorted me to an interview room. He explained to me how the digital interview process was conducted. He also advised me that the interview would be recorded. I thought to myself, *does this kid not realize that*

I used to use the same system? I guess he thought I was a dinosaur and that oldsters like me only knew how to use typewriters.

He started recording and asked me a few questions to loosen me up, like my name, age, address, marital status—almost like a conversation. I expected him to suck at this but he surprised me by being a very good interviewer. He didn't interrupt me while I gave my statement unless he thought he could draw more detail out of me.

I started by giving him my story since I'd left my house, where I'd gone for coffee and so on. This was important so he could check my timelines, get witnesses and exclude me as a suspect. Then I got to the part where I pulled the truck into the laneway. I thought and thought about what to say and asked myself, *what did I actually observe?*

It's tough to remember what you saw when you have no reason to pay attention, and I know from being a cop that witnesses usually only recall about 60 percent of what they observe. I was no different. I made a point of telling Corey how poor the lighting was in the laneway and then I told him about the two men I'd seen and how tall I thought they were. I said I thought the van was a mid- to early-nineties GMC, blue and about six feet high. I noticed both men were about four to six inches shorter than the van roof, making them about five-foot-six to five-foot-eight. Both looked to be Caucasian and had short- to medium-length hair and medium to heavy builds. Both wore pants and coats. One looked like he was wearing a jean jacket, the other a longer fabric coat, plaid, it seemed.

I noticed one more thing about the vehicle, probably because I'm a car guy. The van had some type of yellow sticker on the right rear door glass. I also thought it unusual to have such a large, chrome-coloured thing in the back of the van, as it would likely obscure the driver's rear vision. When my truck's lights shone on it for a few seconds, it definitely caught my attention. I also told Corey that the way that young woman's dress had been pulled up, it was almost a certainty that the victim had been sexually assaulted. And I told him I'd pulled her dress back down.

The interview lasted about an hour and a half. When it was done, I saw Stephanie waiting in the hall to talk to me.

"Hey, Stephanie," I said, "It's been great to see you, though the circumstances could be better. It was nice to help out, but I really have to go get that garbage truck and get it back to the yard."

"Sure, Alex, I understand," she said with a smile. Then, I'm not sure what made me do it, but I asked, "Do you think you might be able to meet with me tomorrow night to talk about the murders?

"You miss being a cop, Alex" she teased. Then, with a smile, she said, "Sure. Drop by the station, around midnight."

"I can do that," I said.

A patrol car gave me a ride back to the scene and I picked up the truck and took it back to the yard. The whole way, my mind was racing a million miles a minute. *What did I see? Did I miss anything? Is this going to help with the investigation? Did the serial killer strike again?* If this murder was related to the other murders, it seemed that there were *two* killers and they were working together.

When I got home I was exhausted and I feel a sleep quickly. I had all these weird dreams about the murders. Then the phone rang and it scared the shit out of me. I jumped up quickly and grabbed it. It was Karen.

"How's it going?" she asked.

"You're not going to believe this," I told her, "I'm a witness in a murder case."

"You're joking!" she said.

I told her about what had happened and she was suitably worried. "Are you okay?" she asked

"Oh, yes. Just tired," I said.

Karen suggested I take the night off, but I told her I couldn't, as Allan didn't have anyone to replace me. I said it was my last night shift and that I would be off for a while after that. Then she reminded me I had a doctor's appointment the following afternoon.

As I got ready for work, I remembered I was meeting with Stephanie later to discuss the murders and I got a little excited. The cop in me was alive and well. However, my other body parts couldn't be relied on. All of a sudden my stomach told me that if I didn't get to the bathroom immediately, I was going to shit myself. I got to the toilet just in time. I had the runs and I also noticed a weird feeling in my left arm. I shook my arm, trying to make it go away. Slowly, it started to fade a little. But it was really uncomfortable.

When I got off the can, I decided to lie down for a few minutes. I had a pain in my neck, at the back, like a nerve was being pinched. I slept for about 45 minutes and felt a lot better when I woke up. I took a couple of aspirin, had some dinner and then off I went to work. At least I had something to look forward to tonight. Stephanie had told me to stop by the station around midnight if I wanted to talk about the murders and I was really kind of excited about that. Knowing it might take a while, I'd even given my boss, Allan, a heads-up. "I might not get the whole route finished tonight," I told him.

"No problem," he said. "Most of the container bins can go a few days without being emptied. If they get too full, the customers can call for an extra pick-up."

At ten minutes to midnight, I pulled into Pete's and grabbed six coffees to take with me to the downtown police station. When I got there, I found Stephanie had left my name with security and so I was escorted to her office immediately. She and Corey were both there and were clearly completely exhausted. By now, they had probably been working for nearly 24 hours straight and, given the media attention, I was betting their bosses were hounding them for updates. This was quite probably the fifth prostitute murdered in less than a year.

"How are you doing?" asked Stephanie as she gratefully took a coffee from me and passed out the others to her team members.

"Fine," I said. "How are you guys?"

"It's been a difficult 20 hours," she told me. "The dead girl has been identified as Cathy Van Hessen, 22 years old, from Bisson City. She's a local girl who started running with a bad crowd. Before she knew it, she was drug addicted and the slippery slope into prostitution followed shortly after that."

Cathy's parents, active and respected community members, had just left the police station. I felt sorry for them, but at the same time I wondered if their social standing might mean more action on these murders. This wasn't some vagrant girl; this was one of Bisson City's own kids.

"How'd the parents take it?" I asked.

"Tough," said Stephanie, as I knew she would. They would never be the same after losing their daughter. Even if someone was arrested and convicted, they still wouldn't ever get their daughter back. Instead of holding out hope, those poor people were selecting a funeral home."

"When will the post-mortem be released?" I asked.

"I think they said a week," Stephanie said.

I thought, *those poor parents probably have so many questions about Cathy's death, the biggest being, why her?*

"So, it's nice of you to drop by," Stephanie said, eyeing me questioningly. Meanwhile, Corey just sort of glared at me. I knew they were both tired and didn't want to entertain someone, even if that someone was a witness. And I was pretty sure I knew exactly what Corey was thinking … *what's this old geezer doing here?*

I dived in. "Listen, guys," I said, "I don't expect to be told any confidential information, but I think I might have some ideas and information that can help catch the killer." They looked at each other, doubtful. "Hear me out before you say anything," I said. "I have been working the night shift in the downtown area for the past year or so and I know a lot of the street people." Then I told them how I had met and helped Sally Armstrong out.

I knew Stephanie was interested. Her ears perked up right away. She and I had always had a connection like that; I had mentored her and she knew that I had once been a skilled homicide investigator. But I wasn't sure what Corey's reaction would be. It only took a few seconds before he asked, "What the hell kind of information could a retired cop find that an entire homicide unit can't?"

I just said, "Just listen to what I have to say. If you're interested in what I know, do one thing for me."

Corey snapped angrily, "And if we do this one thing, will you keep your fucking nose out of our investigation?"

"Settle down and quit swearing, Corey," Stephanie interjected.

It was nice of her to go to bat for me, but I didn't blame Corey. I understood where he was coming from. But I had to put him in his place. I said, "Look, I'm 60 years old with over 30 years of policing experience. I was solving murders when you were in diapers. I know how to do it. But I'm retired and doing something else now. I didn't set out to work on a murder case and really don't need this bullshit. But I know stuff and I'll share it if you want me to."

He grudgingly agreed to listen.

"What I need you to do is check out the murder of a transvestite named Robert—Bobbi—Thompson. Read all the police reports and look closely at the witness descriptions, especially descriptions of the vehicle. Then compare those with descriptions of the vehicle from the Turner homicide. Then, if you get interested in my belief that Thompson could also be a victim of the same killers, let me know. I'm off for three days and back to work on Sunday night."

Corey eyed me appraisingly, but Stephanie, bless her heart, looked grateful.

I made sure they both had my cell phone number and said, "I'll be at Pete's Donuts around midnight on Sunday if you want to meet me there. But only call my cell, as my wife will freak out if she finds out I'm discussing the homicide investigations with you. She's concerned about my health."

I finished the rest of my shift thinking about the investigation, and Corey and Stephanie. I knew where Corey was coming from and that he was really tired from lack of sleep; however, he had to learn to keep an open mind and take information from wherever he could get it. You can't prejudge evidence, or what your witnesses may say. You have to keep an open mind and follow it where it takes you. If you get tunnel vision, you will compromise your investigation.

As usual, I just got home just as Karen was leaving for work. "Don't forget, you have a doctor's appointment at two o'clock," she said on her way out the door. "Make sure to tell him the truth about how you've been feeling. And they should have some of your tests results back. And give me a call as soon as you are done at the doctor's office!" With that, and a kiss, she headed off to work.

I woke up around one o'clock in the afternoon, had a shower and went to the doctor's. I entered old Dr. Sinclair's office and told the receptionist who I was. She said there would be a 15-minute wait and told me to take a seat. I sat down and started looking at some of the other patients, wondering what my test results would be. I could only imagine. A few weeks ago, I'd had some blood and other tests done to determine my heart health, and truth be told, I was a little worried about what the doctor was going to say. I've always tried to look after myself and have worked out regularly since I was a teenager, but I like to eat the wrong things and have lost and gained the same 30 pounds several times in the past ten years. To take it off, I run and lift weights, which is good. But I've also been a drinker my entire life—sometimes too much of one, I confess. And periodically I smoke cigars. My doctor hates that and always tells me to quit.

In my defense, I have worked *years* of shift work, which in itself is unhealthy, and on top of that, being a cop is pretty high on the list of 'most stressful jobs'. I've tried to take it easy since I retired from the police force, and I have been much more relaxed … but in the last few months I haven't felt myself, and even Karen noticed a change in me. She was concerned about my health and that's why I agreed to get the medical tests done.

The receptionist directed me into Dr. Sinclair's office. Although an experienced doctor and a true gentleman, Dr. Sinclair has never kept up with modern technological advances, like computers and electronic filing system. There are hundreds of boxes of files in the hallways and in his office and the carpet, though clean, looks to be about a quarter of a century old.

Dr. Sinclair entered the office, shook my hand and asked, "How have you been feeling?"

I decided I better tell him the truth about what was going on. "Well, doc, I better confess that a little job-related stress has crept back into my life," I said. Then I told him the whole story, complete with my bout with the runs.

"Well, we should probably take your blood pressure again," he said as he made some notes in my file. Then he sat back down at his desk and started reading my medical history. When he was done, he looked at me and said, "Alex, I know your family has a history of heart problems. To be frank, I'm quite concerned about you having a heart attack. Your blood pressure is high and that incident the other day sounds like it might have been a mild heart attack. You did the right thing by taking the aspirin and resting. You should probably do more of that. I want you to go for a complete series of stress tests next week so we can medically evaluate your heart health. You'll be doing physical testing on a treadmill, and you'll get a heart scan. You'll have to do it at the hospital, so get the specialist information from my receptionist before you leave."

Then he said sternly, "Alex, don't fool around with this. I'm really concerned and you should be too. If you start feeling chest pains, tingling in your arm or anything unusual, call an ambulance and get to the hospital."

As I left the office, I knew with certainty that Dr. Sinclair was right. I was in danger. My father died of a massive heart attack in his early 50s and my uncle died of a heart attack in his mid-70s. Congenital heart problems run in my family. And I had most definitely not felt right lately.

When I got home, I grabbed a glass of whiskey and gave Karen a call to tell her what Dr. Sinclair had said. I tried to downplay it a bit, saying, "Dr. Sinclair suggested I lose a few pounds, but otherwise everything is okay." I made a mental note to pick up a couple of bottles of aspirin.

I decided I would take it easy for a couple days, at least until I went back to work Sunday night. Then I wondered if Stephanie and Corey were going to follow up on my suggestion to review the Thompson homicide case files. And I also wondered if they would meet me at the coffee shop.

CHAPTER 4

The next day, then newspapers had a lot of family pictures and stories on Cathy van Hussen. The papers indicated that the homicide task force had expanded to over a hundred police officers. As I had suspected, the murder of *this* girl really stirred things up. Her family was known and well-liked in Bisson City.

I kept seeing images of the victims in my mind and I couldn't believe how similar they all were; nearly the same age, slim builds and blonde hair. Bobbi Thompson was trans but looked the same too and was wearing a blond wig when he died. And Sally Armstrong was black, but she'd died her hair blond and perhaps the night's darkness and her similar build attracted the killers.

I started going for short walks as I waited for Sunday night to arrive and I noticed spring kicking in. It was a little warmer and the snowdrops?snowdrops ? were poking up through the softening ground. It was a nice time of year. I laid low as the doctor suggested but when Sunday finally arrived, as all the regular people went to bed to get for Monday morning, I started my night shift and got ready to talk to Stephanie and Corey.

I drove the truck over to Pete's and as I parked, I noticed that even with all the publicity about the murders, there were still a few girls strolling. However, they appeared more cautious than usual and were watching out for each other and hanging around in groups under the streetlights. Through the open window, I saw once sidle up to a potential customer and tell him through the window, "Uh-uh, we're only doing regulars, sweetie." They were taking care. I was glad.

I hadn't even parked the truck, when through the coffee shop window, I saw Stephanie and Corey sitting at a table. I smirked. They both had 'cop' written all over them.

I went inside, grabbed a coffee at the counter and went over to where they were seated. "Thanks for coming," I said as I sat down with them at the table. "I'm glad you decided to meet me."

Stephanie looked at Corey with a critical eye and said, "Do you have anything to say to Alex?"

Corey looked sheepish, but said, "Listen, I didn't really get that you had so much time on the job and so much experience working homicide investigations." He avoided eye contact as he added. "Maybe I was a little rough with you."

I said, "That's okay, let's get down to business."

He reached out his hand and we shook, then he looked at Stephanie and she said, "Listen, we will talk to you about the murders, but the information we share with you has to stay only with you and remain highly confidential. We could lose our badges if word got out that we discussed evidence with you."

"Of course," I agreed.

She smiled wryly and then said, "I don't imagine it surprises you to know that we believe there is a serial killer, or killers, out there targeting young prostitutes."

"Nope," I said.

Corey pulled out a file folder. "Here's the Robert Thompson murder," he said. "If you're right, he might have been the first, but we didn't catch it because we weren't looking for a serial killer. Bobbi does look similar to the other victims."

He opened the file and started pointing out choice parts to me and we noted the similarities in witness descriptions of the van and the men.

"But it's a different M.O.," said Stephanie, puzzling over the extreme physical trauma to Bobbi's body.

"Not if the attackers became enraged when they found out Thompson's true gender," I said. "That could have provoked a violent attack. Did you identify the weapon used on Thompson?

"The pathologist said probably a large butcher knife for the slashes and cuts, though we never found one. The lab report said an unknown blunt force weapon caused the trauma and bruising."

I asked, "Could it have been someone's fist?"

Corey looked at me. "Not likely. The report didn't specify that the marks were knuckles. But if it was, it came from someone who could really pack a punch. More likely it was a bat or something."

"What about a punch from a boxer or something?" asked Stephanie thoughtfully.

"You never know," said Corey. "But I don't think so."

I said, "I saw *two* men the other night, so if we lump Bobbi Thompson in with the others, then is it it's possible two people murdered him."

"Yes," Stephanie agreed.

Then I said, "I wonder if you guys will answer a few questions for me. If you don't want to answer because it will compromise the investigation, just say so."

They looked at each other and nodded. They were going to play ball.

I started. "Were the hookers sexually assaulted?"

Stephanie answered by nodding 'yes'. Corey confirmed, "Yes, but the specifics are considered hold back evidence."

"Okay," I said, "Great. Now tell me, were the victims suffocated or strangled?"

Corey responded, "Well, the coroner determined that all the causes of death were homicidal suffocation—even Bobbi Thompson, we just found out."

"And what was the method of suffocation?" I probed. "Were they all killed by a bag, like the girl I found?"

Stephanie responded, "Yes. Large, clear plastic bags were put over the victims' heads. Two plastic bags were found at the two laneway crime scenes, near the victims and with victim DNA inside them, probably from their mouths as they gasped for air."

"That's just like the girl I found," I said. "So it's the same M.O. except for the beating of Bobbi Thompson." Then I asked, "Do you have any other information on the vehicle?"

"Well, we got some vehicle paint chips at the Van Hessen crime scene," said Stephanie. "When those guys sped off after you showed up, they banged up a bunch of garbage cans and a guard rail and left chips. Forensics identified the suspect vehicle as a turquoise-blue GMC or Chevy window van, vintage 1990 to1994."

I asked, "Did you get any suspect DNA from any of the crime scenes or victims?"

"No, nothing so far," said Corey.

"No," Stephanie agreed, "But forensic examination of the plastic bags indicated that they were all manufactured by the same company, mass-produced. The same size and thickness with the company logo on the edge ... and of course they were big enough to easily go over the victims' heads."

Then they looked at each other awkwardly, as if they knew something I didn't. I decided to push it. "So you must have something else," I said, "What else do you have? They looked at each uncertainly, but I really wanted to know so I asked again, "Come on, what else do you have?"

Reluctantly, Stephanie answered, "The two victims in the laneway had bread crumbs in their hair. They matched bread crumbs in the plastic bags, or were at least somewhat consistent."

Corey added, "It was the same with Joan White. They found a plastic bag with bread crumbs inside it at the dump site."

Stephanie said, "We don't have much more evidence that we can share. But I can tell you that everybody has been working their asses off ... but these guys are sneaky. We have no clear descriptions and we've had no luck finding more witnesses, so we're paddling in the dark. We haven't received many good tips, either."

"We have all kinds of manpower and resources available to us," Corey added, "But we're not getting any breaks."

"Do you have any ideas, Alex?" asked Stephanie.

I laughed. "I'm glad I'm retired, and these are your cases, not mine. How about you let me think about this for a day or so?. Perhaps we can meet here again around six tomorrow morning when my shift is done," I suggested. "You know me, I'll be mulling this over all night like a crazy guy." Then I said good bye to them and thanked them for following up on the information I had provided. I grabbed another coffee on the way out.

As I reached up for the handle to pull myself into the truck, I felt pain in my left arm again, followed by a tingling sensation. I dropped my coffee as I struggled to get into the truck and then I just sat still in the driver's seat, sweating like a pig. When I could breathe, I took four aspirin and waited. Thirty minutes later I started to feel a bit better and I was able to finish the shift. *Not good, Alex,* I could hear my doctor say. I was kind of worried.

By the time I got home, Karen had already left for work. I was feeling inordinately tired and I was just able to crawl into bed before I passed out. I had a good deep sleep, kind of unusual for me. It's weird, the older a guy gets, the more he has to get up in the night to have a piss. I usually get up every four hours or so, but this time I slept almost nine hours. I woke up with a massive morning erection, which I thought was pretty funny since it was about four o'clock in the afternoon. *This erection is a bonus,* I thought, *I'm just lucky to wake up.*

I watched some television and had something to eat but my mind was elsewhere. I was thinking about Karen and the kids and what I was doing by dipping my finger into policework again. I could feel my stress rising. *Why am I risking everything? I should have called an ambulance or gone to the hospital. My health is a priority, so why am I so involved with these murder investigations? Maybe I'm just stubborn.*

I thought about Kobe, how he used to get me out doing

things, walking, sitting in the backyard. Those things were no longer so much fun without him. He was my buddy. I stared at the urn. "What's up with me, Kobe, old boy?" I asked. I sure missed that dog.

Since my retirement and since Kobe passed, I had become so complacent. I liked the less frantic routine and my comfortable lifestyle, but I wondered, *maybe I'm starved for a challenge and some excitement.* I enjoyed my career as a police officer and I enjoyed going to work every day. My work ethic and dedication got me two promotions as well as the opportunity to work in the homicide unit. Not everyone gets that gig. I got it because I earned it, and because I cared about the job and the people we serve.

I've met many dedicated, hard-working police officers over the years and it's the ones who care who succeed. I remember one homicide investigator who was so highly organized and anal about things that he drove everyone else nuts. But he taught me something I never forgot. He used to say, "Alex, the key to a successful investigation is organization and good communication … and giving a damn." And then he would do something like re-read the same file five times and ask the same questions over and over and make me and everyone else nuts. But it was *that* guy who the brass always put in charge of the most complex, complicated or messed-up homicide investigations. He cared enough to leave no stone unturned. I always thought if a member of my family was ever murdered, I would want a person like him in charge of the investigation.

Then I thought about my garbage job. I was looking forward to work tonight, but it had nothing to do being a trash man. It was because I was going to meet Stephanie and Corey and talk about the murder investigations. It made me feel excited and alive to help. I wanted to bring closure to the victim's families; I want to help arrest the bad guys and make people feel safe. I knew I was no longer an active cop, and that I was just a witness, but it made me feel whole again—useful—to be back on a case, even if I was only a bit player.

I finished the cardboard run and got back to the transfer station as quickly as I could to start the garbage run. Remembering how the stress made my heart act up last time, I took a couple of aspirin before I started the garbage run. Iwasn't sure if it helped or not, but I figured it was better than nothing.

I arrived at the coffee shop before Stephanie and Corey and I grabbed a coffee and headed to the back corner so I could sit with my back to the wall. That's a cop habit that's never left me—in public places, you sit in the corner with your back to the wall so you can observe everyone and everything happening around you and no one can come up behind you.

I looked out the window and saw Stephanie parking her car. She was by herself. I guess Corey was busy, or maybe 6:00 a.m. was too early for him.

As Stephanie ordered her coffee, I snuck a few glances. Although she has aged a bit, she still looks great. She is very attractive and has a great ass. I'm not sure if she's still married or not. She's not wearing a ring. I wonder if she ever had kids. The only thing we've talked about since reconnecting is the murders.

Stephanie sat down. "Hi, Alex," she said. "Corey worked late last night and he won't be in until later. I told him that's okay. It will give you and I a chance to catch up on old times."

I told her, "I only have about an hour before I have to get the garbage truck back to the yard."

"No problem," she said, "I'll talk fast." I always liked her wit.

She asked about Karen and the kids and I gave her a quick update. The kids were a lot younger when Stephanie knew them. At the time they were approaching their teenage years.

"I can't believe they've left home!" she exclaimed. "Where does the time go?"

I asked her if she was still married or had had children. "Oh, you know, that never worked for me," she said. "After my divorce, my career became the main focus of my life. I wanted children, but it never seemed to be the right time. And then this job and the hours I work ... well that was hard on my marriage and it's been hard on relationships ever since. They just don't last. And I'm getting to the point where I don't care. I like my job. I like my life," she said. But she looked a little sad.

Finally we got around to talking about the murders. "What are we missing?" she asked in frustration. "We can't seem to get anywhere. Every bit of information we follow up on eventually dries up. My unit has processed over 2,000 tips in the last year and we still don't have any real, solid leads."

"You're a smart cop," I reassured her. "You're gonna get these guys. But if you ask me, I'd look for local guys. All the murders are so geographically close that I believe the killers are familiar with the area and they either. work, live or pass through it daily. They probably look like they fit right in around here."

She nodded. "I was thinking the same," she said.

"Since the killers seem to have the ability to blend in and travel around without attracting attention, I'd guess they're pretty unassuming guys. That's probably why they were able to abduct and kill the victims so easily. They seem trustworthy and non-threatening. You have to get your people working the streets to catch these guys."

Stephanie said, "What are you talking about? We *have* been working the streets."

"No you haven't. I work down here four nights a week and I have not even *heard* about cops regularly talking to hookers, transients and drunks. Those people are your eyes and ears. Your people have only been scraping the surface."

Stephanie nodded and I could tell her wheels were spinning. I continued, "You have to build trust and rapport with the street people. Your officers have to get down and dirty. Do *not* send cops into the area wearing their blues. Send a guy in scruffy clothes into the downtown areas where the hookers hang out and tell him to befriend them. They are your best witnesses and I'm betting they will help you identify the killers. The may even know who the killers are, but they just don't realize it. Have male and female teams of detectives working together. They can talk to the hookers and go over safety plans with them."

Stephanie interrupted, "We have discussed and implemented safety plans with the girls already," she said.

"Good," I replied, pleased. Then I asked, "So, is there any further information on the unidentified van?"

"No," she said, clearly disappointed. "I had the Ministry of Transportation narrow it down to vans registered in Bisson City, but that's several hundred, and none of them are turquoise. Still, I have someone on it."

The hour passed quickly. I told Stephanie I had to get the truck back to the yard and get home and get some sleep. She said she had to get going too, as she had to get ready for an eight o'clock morning briefing.

"Thanks for your advice, Alex," she said. "It's been great talking." Then she called after me as I started to walk away, "Hey, Alex … do you want to get together tomorrow for lunch or something?"

I was off work, so I said, "Sure." She gave me a business card with her cell number on it and said she would give me a call around eleven in the morning and we could work out when and where. Then she waved good bye and walked away.

When I got home, as usual, Karen was getting ready to go to work. She always dressed so professionally and, looked so pretty. I wolf-whistled her and she smiled.

"Down, boy," she said, then she asked, "How was work?"

I responded, "Pretty quiet."

"That's good," she said. "You need to take it easy. I'm worried about you. Are you sure the doctor said you were okay? You look kind of grey. You need some rest."

I promised her I would get some sleep.

I put myself to bed and got up around two in the afternoon, hoping I'd slept just the right amount to adjust to normal hours. If I don't sleep enough, I end up falling asleep on the couch watching television. I planned to spend the afternoon working on my old, dusty 1966 Plymouth Belvedere. I've had that car for about six years and I absolutely love it. I wouldn't trade it for anything. I have always been interested in cars and I've had Corvettes, Camaros and Firebirds and classic muscle cars over the years. I like tinkering with them and I love driving them. I eventually end up selling them, but I have fun with them before I do. I usually make money on the Corvettes, as long as I look after them.

I wandered into the garage and looked at the Plymouth sitting there. I bought the Plymouth because of memories of my youth; the last car my father bought was exactly like it. The old girl was dusty, so I started polishing her, thinking, *I learned how to drive on this car's twin sister.* Dad taught me how to drive his old Plymouth Belvedere on the dirt roads at the cottage when I about 13 years old and I used to wash his car all the time, just as I am doing now. When he stopped driving, he gave me his car and I drove it until the floor fell out of it. This car even smells the same as my Dad's car, and has a slant six motor, regular brakes and steering, just like his. I even put my Dad's original licence plates and old AM radio on this car, and every time I drive it—or even wash it—I flash back to a time when I was a teenage kid, some 45 years ago.

Washing the car makes me feel calm and I start thinking about my life. It's really bothering me that I haven't told Karen what I've been up to. As I gently stroke the car, I think, *it's about time I sit down and talk to her. Hopefully she won't be too pissed about with me helping with the murder investigations.*

At dinner, I bit the bullet and told her everything. "I didn't really get interested until Sally Armstrong was murdered," I confessed, "But then I started researching the murder cases and meeting and talking with Corey and Stephanie. I'm sorry. I know you want me to take it easy."

Her eyes went wide and she said, "Is that all you have to tell me?"

"Yes," I said. Her eyes suddenly filled with tears. "What's wrong, Karen?" I asked, confused.

"The doctor's office called me at work today. They were concerned that you hadn't booked follow-up tests on your heart," she sniffed. "Why didn't you tell me the truth about your doctor's appointment?"

There was not much I could say. I just looked guilty, and that made her mad.

"You lied to me! Why? Over some stupid murder investigation?"

Still I didn't answer, and she screamed at me, "YOU ARE NOT A COP ANYMORE! I'm retiring next year and I want to travel and enjoy retirement with you. I don't want you to die. The kids and I need you!"

I could hardly speak to Karen now. I was choking back my own tears. "Karen, I have no intention of dying!" I said, hugging her. "I'm sorry to have worried you like this. I guess I just needed to feel like *somebody* again."

I tried to explain my inner feelings, about why I needed to help solve the murders. She didn't care. All she wanted was for me to get treatment for my heart problems and to survive.

"I promise I'll make arrangements tomorrow to have the tests," I told her. Then, both exhausted from talking and crying, we went to bed early and fell asleep in each others' arms. I didn't tell her that deep in my heart, I believed I didn't have that much time left whether I got the tests or not.

The next morning, Karen made me promise once more to phone the hospital and book the tests. I promised, and decided I better not tell her I was meeting Stephanie for lunch.

I called Dr. Sinclair's office to get the specialist's name and phone number and then contacted the hospital to set up tests for the following Friday. They told me to stop by later and pick up the paperwork. The receptionist also told me that I had to be well rested and that I couldn't eat twelve hours before the tests. Then I called Karen and told her the dates and times for my appointments.

When all of that was done, I phoned Stephanie and asked her if we were still on for lunch.

"Yes," she said. "How about we meet halfway to Bisson, near the airport? Are you okay with the Skyway Hotel restaurant?"

"Sure, sounds good," I said. Then I asked, "Are there any new developments with the investigation?" She said she'd talk to me about that at lunch.

I farted around the house for a while, showered and then left to meet Stephanie. On the way, I stopped by Dr. Sinclair's office and picked up the paperwork for my hospital appointment. I was to see a cardiologist named Dr. Burns at the Bisson City Hospital.

As I drove to meet Stephanie, I had mixed feelings about what I was going to tell her. I wanted to stay involved with the murder investigation, but part of me thought, *maybe Karen is right and I should stand down. I'm not a cop anymore. I'm 60 years old—almost 61 years old—with a heart problem.* I was sure Stephanie and Corey didn't really need my help and I wondered if Stephanie was just being polite and talking to me about it for old time's sake. But then I thought it didn't really matter, even if that was the case. I couldn't be the only ex-cop who got excited about rekindling the old cop spirit. Those of us who love the job *always* love the job.

I arrived at the restaurant a few minutes late. Stephanie was already there. She waved at me as I approached the table and said, "Hey, you clean up pretty good." I suddenly realized that the last two times she'd seen me, I'd been in my trash man outfit and I probably smelled like garbage to boot.

"Thanks," I said, suddenly embarrassed. She smiled.

She already had a coffee, so I ordered one too. Then she told me she'd taken my suggestion to put a few cops in plainclothes out on the street to mingle with the street people. "I told them to wear their scrubbiest gear," she said. "I think I have a good team out there now."

"Any luck with information?" I asked.

She said, "Kind of. We picked up some vague details about a male and a female in their 50s approaching hookers. The interesting part is that the female appeared quite masculine and acted butch, so she seemed like a guy until she started talking. That's what we heard."

"That's interesting," I said. "A couple would easily go unnoticed downtown. If people see them out and about late at night, they'd think less of it than if they saw a solo male, that's for sure. That's great information."

"I think so too," she said. "Thanks for kicking my ass to get my guys out on the street."

We ordered a couple of drinks and lunch. I had a salad. I thought of Karen as I turned down the special—fish and chips, one of my favorites. Of course that's what Stephanie ordered; that and some rye. Stephanie was one of the few females I knew who could drink rye just like one of the guys. When we worked together, at the end of the day we used to get together and knock back a few as we discussed the investigation, before heading off our separate ways.

After a couple of drinks I finally had the courage to ask Stephanie if I was being a pain in the ass by sticking my noise in her investigation. I explained that I just wanted to help out, but I had no intentions to interfere.

Stephanie sat back in her chair, gave me a cool gaze, and said, "Listen, Alex … originally Corey thought you were sticking your nose where it didn't belong but when he listened to your questions and ideas he realized something I've known for years—that you have a lot of knowledge and excellent investigative skills. Plus you care about others and want to help people."

I was flattered. "Thanks, Stephanie," I said.

She went on, "I know you're retired, but it's clear you still have the passion, determination and drive to work on complicated investigations. Alex, I learned so much from you when I first started investigating homicides. That was a great growing opportunity for me and I owe you a lot. Because of you, and what I learned from you, I became the first female homicide inspector in the history of the Bisson City police service."

I didn't know what to say. Her words meant so much to me. She understood the impact she was having and said, "Alex, don't ever think you are interfering with this investigation. I always remember what you told me about how to conduct homicide investigations. You said you can't have tunnel vision and you have to keep an open mind to any source of information that may assist in the investigation. And you taught me that a good leader believes in communication and teamwork."

I was surprised at that comment. She sounded just like me! I said, "Thanks, Stephanie. You have matured into a great homicide investigator."

Then suddenly Stephanie moved forward and before I knew it she kissed me on the lips, her soft little tongue darting into my mouth. Her lips were so soft and her perfume smelled so nice and although we only kissed for a few seconds, it seemed like an eternity. I hadn't been kissed like that for years.

Almost as quickly she moved away from me and said, "Hey Alex, let's get a bottle and room."

My mind started racing a mile a minute. When I used to work with her, I often fantasized about her body, and having wild sex with her. I imagined being with her would be hot and explosive, and that we would ravish each other like a couple of young, horny teenagers ... but I never thought it would happen, let alone that she would make the first move. My fantasies were just that—fantasies. Outside of my horn-dog mind, I acted and the part of father figure and I was sure she saw me that way too.

Then my brain came to a standstill as I started thinking about my age and heart condition. If I got that excited, I would probably have a massive heart attack and die. *But what a great way to go.*

I grabbed her hand, flustered, and said, "Stephanie, as much as I want to, I just can't. I'm married and I love Karen. You've just offered me something I fantasized about for years … but it was just thoughts. You deserve to be with someone younger, who loves you and wants to be with you for the rest of your life, and that can't be me."

I hated saying it, but I had to. I wondered if I'd said too much. She didn't ask me to marry her; she just wanted to get fucked. She looked disappointed and said sadly, "It's okay, I understand." Then with sad, puppy-dog eyes, she said, "I'm sorry for kissing you."

"Don't feel sorry for kissing me," I said. "I enjoyed it, and if it was a different time in our lives, my answer would have been different."

Stephanie said, "So what happens between us now?"

With a smirk, I said, "I have always known that you're a beautiful person with a great ass. Now I know you also have soft lips and a wild little tongue." She looked a little embarrassed, so I squeezed her hand and added, "Nothing changes. We are friends, and if I can, I want to help you catch a couple of serial killers."

CHAPTER 5

As I drove home, I wondered if I had made the right choice in not sleeping with Stephanie. For nearly 30 years, Karen had always been there for me, through the shift work, the long hours and all the missed family gatherings. She'd put up with my drinking and how I sometimes brought home work-related stress; at times we had trouble communicating, but we were able to stay together and accomplish a lot through the good and bad times. We enjoyed life together and raised two beautiful children.

I glanced over at the medical forms on the passenger seat next to me. *Yes, you made the right decision,* I told myself. I was pretty sure Stephanie would have killed me in the sack. Then I started to think about what Stephanie would look like with no clothes on. I was sure she had a beautiful, firm body.

I arrived home and as I walked into the house Karen greeted me. "How was your day, hon?" she asked.

I handed her the medical forms and told her, "Not bad. I had lunch with a buddy I used to work with." She didn't ask more and I didn't say more. But I felt a bit guilty.

We decided to have dinner in the living room and watch the six o'clock news. It started with a flash announcement that another female's body had just been found in the downtown core of Bisson City. I stopped eating momentarily. I couldn't believe it. It seemed the killings were escalating.

The story started to roll and showed a taped-off area along the harbour front. It looked like the warehouse area east of the river mouth, but I wasn't sure. A police spokesperson indicated that they were in the early stages of the investigation and that a task force designated to solve what was now being dubbed the 'prostitute murders' had taken over the investigation.

There was a large group of media at the scene and I could see Corey and Stephanie talking to other investigators in the background. The reporters had already tied the newly-discovered body to the other murders and had further made the logical leap that the police had little to go on, or this killing would not have occurred. It didn't look good for Stephanie and Corey. The media was speculating that 'police were hopeful' the killers had left evidence behind this time. Locating DNA at the scene and matching it to the DNA databank would be huge step for the investigation.

As I watched the tube, I noticed beyond the police tape, in the background, there was Old Joe with his buggy full of various bags. *Interesting*, I thought. I recalled from my police days, before I ever got to know him, that Old Joe used to periodically get busted hanging around that warehouse when the temperature dropped. There was a steam pipe running through that area, part of the old downtown train yard. Old Joe and some of the other homeless guys camped by it as a way to stay warm in the cold Ontario winters.

I remember one particularly nasty day while I was still on a cop—in the hard months, January or February—when I was checking out a stolen, abandoned vehicle down there. As I looked the vehicle over for damage, I was freezing my balls off, and then I looked over and saw Joe sitting on the steam pipe, shaving. I didn't know his name or anything about him at that time, but back then some of the other cops called him 'Steam Pipe Joe' because he lived on the steam pipe. He was right cozy, too. He'd built a shed out of some old pieces of plywood and put a blue tarp over it, complete with a clothes line. It was about as comfy as a guy could get living on the street. I knew the railroad cops use to chase him off the railroad property, but I left him alone. He wasn't hurting anyone, and truth be told, I admired his ingenuity.

I better let Stephanie and Corey know about him, I thought. *He might have seen something and could be a good witness.* I sent Stephanie an email, thought I didn't expect to hear back.

I enjoyed the next couple of days, off work, lounging about the house. Periodically, I followed the news stories on the latest murder. The media said police were having a difficult time identifying the victim, and for now the media was calling her Jane Doe. *Sad that she isn't missed by anyone,* I thought.

I contacted Dr. Burns' office and confirmed my appointment. The receptionist said she'd received my medical records from Dr. Sinclair and that Dr. Burns wanted to do further medical tests on me at the Bisson City Hospital. I wrote down all the instructions she gave me on a piece of paper.

Soon it was Sunday evening and time to get back to work. I hadn't bothered Stephanie or Corey in the last couple of days as I knew that with the new homicide they would be overwhelmed with work and I didn't want to be a pest. Despite Stephanie's reassurance that she welcomed my input, I know cops can be pretty territorial about their cases and Corey had that little edge. I didn't want to cross it. I also knew Stephanie would be extremely busy managing the show. There are a lot of moving pieces in a murder investigation. She's the boss and is responsible for the speed, flow and direction of the investigation. She puts the players in their places and manages them all. She deals with the brass, the media and the victims' families, although not directly, but she has to make sure they're kept in the loop. She'd been working on these murders for a year and in the last six months, when it was confirmed she had a serial killer, or killers, on her hands, things had really ramped up. Now she was flat-out and not only did she have to keep her staff of investigators, warrant writers, technical support and surveillance teams from burning out, but she had to try not to burn *herself* out. She was managing a large task force … but if anyone could manage such an investigation, it would be Stephanie.

Just before I left for work, I gave Stephanie a quick call to see if she had time for a coffee. She sounded very groggy when she picked up. "I finally just got to bed," she told me.

"Sorry to wake you up," I apologized. "Do you want me to let you get back to sleep?"

"No, it's okay. I had to get up anyway," she said.

"I just wanted to know how the investigation is going. I saw the news," I told her.

"Overall, it's still slow," she admitted. "We still haven't identified the last victim. I think she's from out of town and new to prostitution. But she fits the victim profile, early 20s and long blonde hair."

"Sounds like it," I said. Then I told her, "I saw you and Corey on the news."

"Yeah, we figure that's the dump site," she told me.

"I also saw a homeless guy I know on the news," I said. "He showed up behind you guys when you were talking to the press. I'm wondering if any of your people talked to him." I described Old Joe to her.

"Old Joe?" she asked. "Does he have a real name?"

"That's for your guys to figure out," I told her. "But I'm thinking Old Joe could be a witness. He lives down there, especially in the winter. He knows every nook and cranny of that place, and if someone was there, he probably saw them. Plus he knows a lot of people in the downtown area. Somebody should track him down and see if he knows anything about the murders. I haven't seen the guy for a while, but he's out there."

"Okay, Alex. I appreciate the tip," Stephanie said. We finished talking and she said she would call me later.

For my next four trash man shifts, as I drove the trash truck around I kept my eyes open for Joe, or anything suspicious. I didn't hear from Stephanie and I wondered if they had located him and if he'd seen anything. I hope they at least *tried* to track him down. I finished my fourth shift on Wednesday night and I was just getting into my pickup truck to drive home, when my cell rang. It was Stephanie. She sounded very excited as she said, "We've finally located Joe ... and guess what? He witnessed two people dumping that girl into the river!"

"You're kidding!" I exclaimed.

"No! And he made a statement. I don't' want to tell you what we got from him over the phone. Can you come down to the station?"

I said, "For sure, I just finished work. I can be there in about 15 minutes."

Before the call, I was tired and about to go home and sleep, but now I was wide awake and excited. I wondered what Joe had seen and what direction the murder investigation might take because of it.

When I arrived at the police station, Stephanie and Corey were in the lobby waiting for me. They quickly ushered me upstairs into the homicide unit office.

"Take a seat, Alex," Stephanie said, so I did. "You're not going to believe this. First of all, it took my team just about two days to find Joe. He's not an easy guy to track down! But when they found him, he was pretty good about talking to them and he's a lot more eloquent than they expected, too. He told them he saw a mid-size window van in the area, near the river. He originally thought it was a couple parking and making out, but then he saw the sliding door on the passenger side open. The driver grabbed the victim's ankles and pulled her out, and then the passenger grabbed her shoulders. Joe saw them carry her about five feet to the river's edge and then they threw her in. He also said the victim had something over her head and that it looked like a plastic bag."

"Did she?" I asked.

"Yup," said Stephanie. "She had a plastic bag over her head, tied around her neck."

"Just like the girl I found," I said. I looked at Corey, who was squirming around like a little kid in a candy store. He couldn't keep still. Finally, he said, "Inspector, can I tell him?"

"Go ahead," said Stephanie.

He looked at me and said, "Joe thought he recognised the vehicle and the two suspects. He thought they were hot dog venders who worked a cart downtown."

"So we've started looking into all the licenced vendors in the city," Stephanie cut in.

"Big job," I commented. I knew it there must be at least a thousand licenses they were going to have to review and I knew how daunting this might be. Bisson City's by-law office had a list of everyone who had even *applied* for a business licence; hot dog carts, ice cream carts, small-sized food trucks and even catering trucks had to be licensed. Most licences only had a numbered company name or one owner's name on them, so it would be hard to pinpoint individual operators.

"I know, but it's a start," said Corey. "We have a team of detectives reviewing all the city's business licence applications right now."

"Do you think you could spend the day with us visiting various hot dog vendors?" asked Stephanie. "Maybe you can ID the van if you see it."

I said, "As much as I love hot dogs and the idea of cruising around eating them all day, the truth is I only saw that vehicle from a distance. I'm not sure if I can help you much."

Corey then said to Stephanie, "Come on, tell him!"

Stephanie said, "Hey Alex, you must be getting old."

"What do you mean?" I asked.

"What's a hot dog cart look like? What colour is it and what is it made of?"

"I dunno, probably some type of steel or aluminum." Then I

got what they were trying to tell me. I said, "Holy shit! The van had a shiny hot dog cart inside it and that's what my headlights hit!"

Corey and Stephanie nodded approval and then Stephanie asked, "What else comes to mind?"

I thought, *I must be really tired, as I don't really understand what they're talking about.* Then they both said at the same time, "Hot dog and hamburger buns come in plastic bags. The bags are large from bulk purchases ... and bread crumbs are usually left in the bags."

I got pretty excited and then suddenly I felt such incredible pain shoot up my arm and across my chest that I completely blacked out. When I woke up a few minutes later on the floor, there were a few worried police officers standing around me. Stephanie was really upset. "Are you okay?" she asked. "Should I call an ambulance?"

"I'm okay," I muttered, embarrassed and weak. "I'm just tired and I didn't eat much today," I lied. "No ambulance. I'm okay."

"Are you sure?" asked Stephanie. "I don't think you're okay to drive home. Let me call a cab, at least."

"No, I'm fine," I lied again as I struggled to my feet with the assistance of some healthy, strong young men.

I could tell she didn't believe me, but that she didn't want to contradict me or tell me what to do. She frowned as she said, "Be careful driving home ... and get a sandwich or something. Then get a good sleep, okay?"

I nodded. "For sure," I said.

She softened, knowing how much I enjoy the chase of a good homicide investigation. "I'll be in touch if anything develops with the hot dog cart information," she told me. I nodded my thanks and she added, "We're going to set up some surveillance teams to monitor people working vending carts near the crime scenes. We're also going to drive Joe around the downtown area to see if he recognises any of the hot dog venders or their vehicle."

"That's good news," I said. Then I said good bye and left.

As soon as I was out of sight I popped some aspirin and stopped to take a breather. Though I was anxious and confused, I was pretty sure I'd been able to fool Stephanie and Corey and anyone else who witnessed that shameful moment of weakness. But now that I was alone, I was really concerned about my heart. I was pretty sure I'd had a mild heart attack and I knew the best thing to do was to get home and get some sleep. My specialist appointment was tomorrow and I fully expected to hear that I had a serious heart condition. The attacks were getting a stronger and more painful and I was ashamed to realize I'd been in full denial about the severity of the problem and that it would probably be confirmed soon.

I popped aspirin like candy and most of the pain left. I managed to get home and crawl into bed and I awoke somewhat refreshed, though still a little scared. Karen was already at work, so I made myself a coffee and re-read the pre-test instructions I had received. *I hope the doctor doesn't find out about this mornings attack,* I thought. The next morning n I made way to the Bisson City Hospital to see Dr. Burns.

The receptionist escorted me into the doctor's office. I sat in a chair in front of Dr. Burns' desk. He certainly had a lot of diplomas on his wall and the dates on them suggested he'd been practising medicine for a while.

Dr. Burns entered the office. We shook hands and he cut to the chase right away, saying, "Alex, we are going to do a few more tests on you. My preliminary thoughts are that you have developed a serious heart problem. I'm not exactly sure what's going on, but you probably have some partially blocked arteries, and if so, you should consider surgery—and soon."

He went on to tell me that the preliminary tests conducted by Dr. Sinclair had shown plaque clogging up my artery walls and reducing blood flow to my heart. "Blocked arteries cause the heart to not get enough blood, and then heart attacks and heart failure occur," he said. "Surgery is required when more than 70 percent of the artery is blocked, unless, of course, a patient has a medical condition that doesn't allow that. I can prescribe medication for you until further tests can be completed, but if the tests show artery blockage, then by-pass surgery is required and stints will be placed around your heart to help with blood flow."

I nodded my understanding.

"For today, however, all I need is for you to fill out some paperwork. I'll write a prescription for you and we'll take some blood for some further testing." Then Dr. Burns took his glasses off and looked directly into my eyes. He said, "Alex, this is a very serious situation. You could have a heart attack and die. You need to avoid stress and you should try to lose some more weight."

"Okay," I said, worried.

"I'll have my receptionist call you and schedule an appointment. And don't forget to tell your wife about your condition so she can assist you if anything happens." I nodded again and he finished with, "If you experience any type of heart attack symptoms, call 911 and get into the hospital immediately."

I left the office, not surprised by the results. Although I'm not in bad shape for my age, I know I have not led a healthy life style over the years. *I guess all my bad habits are finally catching up to me,* I thought.

On the drive home, I started looking back over my life. I wasn't ready to die yet, but if I wasn't careful, I would. I didn't want to lose everything I'd worked for and held dear. *I have been very fortunate in my life. I have a beautiful wife and two great children. I have a nice home. I have great memories. I've been a good provider,* I thought. But I was also aware that I could have been a better husband and father, and I felt some regret about that. Sometimes I got my priorities mixed up. Family is supposed to be the number one thing in life, but at times I got so wrapped up in my work that it took over my life. I worked horrendous hours on murder investigations and then I'd come home and all I could think about was the investigation, gathering evidence, the victim's family and so on. And the long hours were killer. Sometimes when I got home I had just enough time to get a couple of hours of sleep, shower and drive back to work. Sometimes I had a few drinks to escape all the stress for just a few hours. It was the only way I knew how to ease the pressure, if only for a short period of time.

Policing is one of those professions that can take control of who you *are*. It can make you bitter and twisted if you let it. Police officers are exposed daily to situations full of violence and trauma. Officers are only called to bad situations, when people need assistance because they're hurt, angry, threatened or wronged. No one ever calls the police when things are going right.

At times, over the years, I let it get to me and I felt bad about that. In retrospect, family should been a higher priority, my first priority, and policing, my job, should have been second. But it didn't always work like that. I did help Karen with raising the kids, and I did do things for Karen, but sometimes I was absent even when I was physically there. Nevertheless, I *tried* to be a good father and husband—and I tried to look after myself, though today's diagnosis would say different. I have exercised just about every day since I was a kid of 20. I've lifted a lot of weights over the years and done some cardio training too. My weight went up and down a lot, though, usually because of the stress and the drinking. I've gone as high as 260 pounds and as low as 220. At 220, I felt and looked good but I always thought a strong wind might blow me over.

I sighed. I was sure my eating habits, drinking, and weight fluctuations hadn't helped my heart much. *Well, it can't be helped now,* I thought. I decided to go home, get some sleep and then tell Karen about what Dr. Burns had said when she got home.

I slept for about five hours. When I heard the garage door opening, I got out of bed, went downstairs and greeted Karen with a kiss. "How was your day?" she asked.

"The good news or the bad?" I asked.

I didn't have to say much more. Her face told me that she knew what the doctor had told me. But I told her anyway. She started to cry and I hugged her. "I'm sorry," I said.

"Why would you say that?" she asked through her tears.

"Listen," I said, "I believe what goes around comes around and over the years I've neglected not only my health, but our family too. There were times when I put myself before you guys, and I regret it now."

"Alex, don't," she said tearfully.

"I have to, Karen. I don't think I am going to survive my heart problems."

Karen reached over and held my hand. "There are a lot of people who survive heart surgery," she said. "And you will too. And please don't beat yourself up. No one is perfect and though we've had some issues over the years, we've stayed together and we have a great life, beautiful kids, a nice home ... and each other."

I told her about my medication and that I would require further tests. "Dr. Burns said there is a good chance I will have to have by-pass surgery."

"Quit your job," said Karen firmly. "We don't need the extra money. You should concentrate on your health."

"You're right," I agreed. "I'm going to quit my job in a few weeks, sooner if Allan Featherstone can find another night driver to replace me."

We discussed when I should schedule the next doctor's appointment, and Karen said, "Soon. And once we get the test results back we're going to tell the kids. We're in this as a family, Alex."

We watched television for a while and then went to bed, but I couldn't sleep. I couldn't believe it. Here I was, having just received life-altering news about my health, but instead of thinking about my heart condition, I was mulling over the homicide investigations and wondering if Stephanie and Corey had any more news. *You're an idiot, Alex*, I thought.

I got up the next morning and had a coffee with Karen. I hate to admit it, but I was waiting for her to leave so I could phone Stephanie and get an update. I could have texted her, but I'm old school. Texting takes too long and there're all those tiny little keys to push. The phone is a lot quicker and easier.

As soon as Karen left, I called her. "Things are starting to move fast," she said excitedly. "Can you meet me at the police station in about an hour?"

I said, "Sure." Then I had a quick shower and went downtown. I felt pretty good and thought the medication Dr. Burns had given me must be helping. But I still knew I needed to slow down if I wanted to be around for Karen and the kids.

As I drove toward the station, I told myself, *after this, that's it. I have to remove myself from this murder investigation. I have to stop this for my health.*

CHAPTER 5

I got to the police station just after ten in the morning and Stephanie met me in the lobby. I followed her to her office.

"I've had some good news," she said. "Researching the vendor licences, and some good surveillance work, paid off. My investigators identified a husband and wife team who have hot dog cart licences for two downtown locations. There are two surveillance teams on them now."

She told me they had been identified as Angelo Martino, age 55, and Sophie Martino, age 50. "And guess what?" she asked me

"What?" I replied.

"The surveillance team said they meet the descriptions we've got. Both have stocky, heavy builds and should-length, greying hair—and according to Joe, she looks like a man!"

"Whoa, that explains a lot," I said. The downtown hookers are more likely to trust a guy if he's got a woman with him."

"Uh huh," said Stephanie, "And to make it even sweeter, Angelo has a 1995 Chevrolet window van registered to him," she continued. "We reviewed *your* statement and the surveillance team thinks the shiny thing you saw through was the hot dog cart, like we guessed. They took pictures of them loading that thing into the rear of the van with a folding ramp system. They also videoed the reflections of their headlights on it—just like what you saw. And they photographed a yellow ribbon sticker in the corner of the rear passenger side window."

"That's awesome, Stephanie. You got the bastards now!" I yelped.

Corey came into the office and interrupted our conversation. "We just got two arrest warrants," he said, "And search warrants too, for the van, the hot dog carts and the Martino residence at 367 DuPont Street, Bisson City.

"Congratulations, guys," I said to Stephan and Corey.

"Thanks, man," said Corey. "But it's not over yet."

"The case looks pretty strong to me," I said. "I'm thinking that soon you and the team should be able to wrap it up."

"Yup," said Stephanie. "We've been busy. Part of the team worked on an arrest plan and others worked on the search warrants. I'm really proud of them for getting that paperwork done so quickly!"

"That's great," I said. "The citizens of Bisson City will be happy and feel safer when you make the arrests."

"On that note," said Stephanie hesitantly. "We're ready to execute the arrests. Do you want to go for a ride with us and watch from a distance?"

I sure did. I *more* than wanted to, but I simply said, "Sure, thanks. Is it okay?"

"I can justify your involvement because you're an eye witness," she said. "You can help us recognize the suspects and their vehicle." I smiled as she said, "Let's go! We already have both plainclothes and uniform officers in the area ready to make the arrests."

We left the police station in an unmarked police van and parked just down the street from where the Martinos were serving food from their hot dog cart near the corner of Vermont Drive and Devine Street so we had a good seat. We saw their van parked just in the laneway east of Vermont Drive, north of Dundas Street. I couldn't believe the two of them were so casually working so close to the scenes of their crimes.

I sat in the back of the van, listening to the massive amount of chatter on the police radio. Corey's and Stephanie's cell phones rang every few minutes and it was apparent they were coordinating their arrest plan. It was just approaching noon, the busiest time of day at one of the busiest intersections in Bisson City. Both Martinos were working hard, barbequing hot dogs and hamburgers for the lunch time crowd. There were all kinds of people near the intersection of Vermont Drive and Devine Street, but Stephanie pointed out a couple of detectives in old, baggy sweats approaching the Martinos. Quickly, four more detectives in suits also approached.

Stephanie yelled into her radio, "Greenlight, greenlight go, go!" and the group of officers surrounded the suspects quickly and quietly. In a matter of seconds, the two most wanted serial killers in the history of the city were arrested. I'm sure the 100 or so people waiting to cross the intersection had the shit scared out of them as plainclothes officers, uniform patrol and tactical officers flooded the area. I know the people lined up at the Martinos' cart sure did.

Soon, the entire area was sealed off around the intersection, including the immediate area around the hot dog cart and the laneway where the van was parked. Yellow police tape went up everywhere to protect potential evidence and the Martinos were searched and whisked away in separate police cars.

"You did a great job," I told her warmly as we watched the Martinos being driven away. "You should be very proud. You done good, kid," I told her.

She smiled at me. "You helped," she said.

Because she and Corey were about to get very busy interviewing the accused, executing search warrants and dealing with swarms of media, Stephanie said she'd drop me off at my truck and call me in a few days. I knew her team still had a lot of work to do. They had to gather evidence and prepare for one of the biggest court cases in the history of the city.

As I drove home in rush hour traffic, pleased with the events of the morning, I was suddenly struck by the fact that, despite all the excitement, the old ticker had held firm. *The medication must be doing a good job*, I thought. But then I remembered I was supposed to be taking it easy today, that I'd promised Karen I wouldn't overdo it—and *that* stressed me out. I had to beat her home before she found out I was out. I stepped on the gas.

I managed to beat Karen home in time to clean up and barbeque some chicken for dinner. I sat down in front of the television to watch six o'clock news, eager to check out what the media had to say about the arrests. The arrests were the top story on every news station. The reporters interviewed the police chief and the mayor, both of who gave credit to their homicide unit and referenced Stephanie's leadership and the team's dedication and hard work during the past two years. Then Inspector Stephanie Foster took the stage and made a statement, professionally answering all questions and looking great to boot. She said both accused would be attending bail court the next morning and at that time their names would be released to the public. She also said that each accused would be charged with seven counts of first-degree murder.

I knew that to lay a first-degree murder charge, planning and intent must be proven and I was sure Stephanie's team had consulted with prosecutors already. The hard work in a homicide investigation starts *after* the arrests. The burden is on the police to prove guilt and if the killers don't confess or provide statements, it makes things difficult. Then the prosecutor has to decide whether to try them together or separately. Separate trials are a huge expense to the province, and it takes forever to prosecute each case. I had been wondering how the prosecutor would handle it. Now I knew.

Karen walked in through the garage door and immediately said, "I heard there was an arrest in the serial killings."

I said, "Yes, I was just watching it on TV."

"That Stephanie cop you used work with was on the news," she commented.

"Yes, I saw her."

"Even without your involvement, they were able to make arrests," she said drily.

I said, "Yes, you are right."

Karen asked, "Do you think you will have to go to court and testify?"

"Probably," I said. "But I can't identify the accused. I could barely see them in the dark and I only saw their vehicle from a distance. But I can identify the body, though. And I saw the yellow ribbon sticker on the van window. And the silver hot dog cart in the rear of the van. But I'm not sure if the case will go to trial. Two accused and multiple criminal charges is a lot for the prosecutor to take on. I'm betting a deal or plea gets worked out with one of them."

"Well, if they did it, I hope they get locked up for good," she commented as she got some chicken off the barbeque.

That night I got a phone call from Allan Featherstone. He told me if I still wanted to quit that he'd found a night driver to replace me. I said, "Yes, I'm ready to pack it in."

"Well, we're gonna miss you, Alex," he said. Then he said the new driver could start right away and I told him that was great.

"I'll be down in the next couple of days to clean out my locker," I said.

"No rush," said Allan. "And then lets you and me go out for lunch and a couple of drinks."

When we hung up, and being the bloodhound that I am, I thought, *maybe when I go down to see Allan I can contact Stephanie for an update on the investigation.* I wondered if either Martino had provided a statement, and if any evidence had been found in the van or in their house.

I waited a couple of days and gave Stephanie a call. She indicated that the investigation was moving along well, but there were a few investigative hurdles to get over. She said she would tell me about it later. I was kind of anxious to find out what was going on. We arranged to meet for lunch.

I went outside and started raking up the leaves, but I struggled with the exertion and noticed that I seemed to be sweating a lot. I immediately slowed down and took my time, all the while thinking about how many times I have raked the leaves, cut grass and shovelled snow in this old yard of mine. It was also a great place to throw the ball for Kobe. At the thought of Kobe, I grew wistful. I sure missed that happy dog.

Before I knew it, I was out of breath. I sat down in a lawn chair. I knew I had to watch it. I needed those heart tests as soon as possible, and if I was ever going to see my kids get married, I probably needed heart surgery too—as soon as they could book me, from the sounds of it. Dr. Burns and Dr. Sinclair had both mentioned that they thought I should try to lose some more weight while I waited and prepared for potential surgery. I thought, *good luck with that, Alex…* but I would at least *try* to drop a few pounds.

That night when Karen got home, the first thing she said when she saw all the bagged leaves was, "You shouldn't have raked up the leaves. You should be taking it easy!" She was right, of course. But somehow I resented her saying so.

The next day, I called Stephanie around nine-thirty. "I'm kinda busy and can't get out for lunch," she said. "How about you come by my office around eleven?"

"See you then," I said. Then I called Allan Featherstone and told him I would stop by his office around two in the afternoon.

"Sure, Alex," he said. "And after you clean out your locker we can go out for a couple of beers and some wings." I told him that would be nice.

I was sorry to stop working for Allan. In all the years I have known him, I've admired him for being the kind of guy who knows when to take a break from work and get away for a few beers and some wings. He is very social and can always entertain a crowd with funny stories. I was going to miss working for him.

I arrived at the police station right on time and was escorted by a uniformed officer to Stephanie's office. I think the officer was surprised when she greeted me with a big hug. *What? A homicide inspector is actually a human who can give hugs?*

"That officer looked shocked when you hugged me," I commented.

She laughed. "I wonder what he would have done if I had kissed you?"

I thought, *he and I would* both *have had a heart attack*!

She told me that she had to step out for a couple of minutes and as I sat in her office I thought about the young police officer I had worked with so many years ago and how she was now one of the most well-respected homicide inspectors in the entire police service, and probably the province. She was highly skilled, well trained, professional, sociable and a skilled case manager who had led an investigative team to solve a string of serial killings, elevating her policing status to a new level. It wouldn't surprise me if she climbed the corporate ladder to the level of police chief. A lot of previous police chiefs had come from the homicide unit. All that and she was also *hot*.

Stephanie returned to the office and when she walked past me I couldn't help checking her butt out again. It still looked great. Some guys are boob guys, but I liked firm butts.

"I have a lot to tell you," Stephanie said. "First of all, thanks for helping me."

"No thanks required," I told her. "You ran the investigation and you and your team deserve all the credit. I'm a witness and a tipster, that's all." I couldn't wait any longer, so I asked, "Well, did they talk?"

She said, "Both provided self-serving statements and pointed the finger at each other. They had similar stories about immigrating to Canada from Italy. They came from the same village in Sicily."

She told me their parents were neighbors who, during the German occupation of their village in 1942, were exposed to horrific war crimes, and then later were affected by economic difficulties caused by the war's aftermath. The families decided to immigrate to Canada together in the early 1960s. They wound up at the west end of Bisson City, near Wellington Street and St. Clair Avenue, neighbors and friends to this day. Angelo and Sophie eventually started dating and got married, but they had no kids. According to Stephanie, Sophie claimed to have been abused as a child and manipulated by Angelo.

"I get the picture," I said as she told me their story. It's no secret to us cops that in the 1960s and 1970s, there were a lot of family secrets. Domestic and sexual abuse, usually fueled by alcohol, were common and the scars affect society to this day.

"Sophie's claim is where the stories diverge," said Stephanie. "Angelo portrays *himself* as a victim who was physically abused and controlled by *Sophie*. He said Sophie used to be a beautiful, loving woman. He also said that sometime in the last few years, he made a huge mistake ... and that Sophie caught him with a young, blonde hooker. According to him, she never forgave him for his indiscretion."

"Well, that would explain why they target blondes," I commented.

"There's more," said Stephanie. "Sophie was never able to have children, so she started drinking and gaining weight. He says she was abusive when she was drunk, and would beat him up. At first, it was only with her fists, but it escalated until she was using both fists *and* weapons. He said one time she stabbed him with a knife and he had to get stitches."

"Nasty," I said.

"He confessed to being at the scenes of the crimes, but insists the attacks were planned by Sophie and that it was *her* who approached the girls and lured them to locations where they could be killed, suffocated with plastic bags, to be precise. A couple of times, he said, Sophie made *him* kill them threatening to beat him up or otherwise torture him if he refused."

"She sounds like a piece of work," I commented, thinking of my sweet Karen and counting my blessings.

"Angelo further told investigators Sophie kept a metal rod in the hot dog cart and would beat him with it when he didn't obey her. According to his statement, Sophie was so enraged about him having sex with the blonde hooker that, not only did she target blonds, but she sodomized some of the victims with the same metal rod."

"Ouch," I said, wincing a little. "Can that be proved?"

"Yes, we found the rod, just as he said, and conducted DNA testing on it. Three of the victims' DNA profiles matched DNA found on the metal rod. I never discussed this part of the case with you before because it was hold back evidence, but I'm sure you've figured out by now that post-mortems on three of the victims showed trauma and excessive tearing to their vaginal and anal areas consistent with the violent insertion of a hard, blunt object."

I just shook my head at the brutality of it all. Then I asked, "So what did Sophie say?"

"Pretty much what you'd expect," said Stephanie with a sigh. "She said *she* was the victim and that she was regularly beaten and sexually abused by her drunken husband. She totally blamed him and said he forced her to participate in the killings. She said if she didn't help him lure the victims to their van, Angelo beat her, and that one time he beat her so badly he just about killed her. She said she was in the hospital for weeks with broken ribs, a concussion and a broken arm. And she said Angelo used the metal rods on the girls because he was too drunk to get an erection!"

"Well, her story should be easy to check out," I said. "There would be hospital records from a stay that long. Was it the Bisson City Hospital?"

"She said she couldn't remember what hospital it was, so we've executed search warrants all the hospitals in a fifty-mile radius to obtain both Angelo's and Sophie's medical records. Investigators also interviewed their neighbors and located a few of their friends and interviewed them all. All the information we have so far indicates they've been beating on each other for years."

"Wholesome couple," I commented.

Stephanie smirked. "One of the neighbors said they were both power drinkers and that they usually started in the early morning hours. He said they argued a lot and that their fights usually ended in violent, physical brawls. Another neighbor said the same. Apparently both Martinos are alcoholics with violent tempers."

She added, "We pulled all the police records on the two of them and found out there have been 30 callouts to their place in the last year—for noise complaints, ambulance, domestic dispute and assault. And they also got nailed for a couple of drunken incidents at a bar near their home. Apparently Sophie tried to punch out the bartender because he wanted to stop serving her liquor as she was too drunk. Police pulled the video from the bar and it was clear she was the aggressor. But you know what's weird? I looked at that video and had a really hard time telling the two of them apart. It's uncanny how similar they look from behind. Little brick shithouses, the two of them. Solid and thick."

Maybe they're narcissists and are in love with their own images," I remarked.

"Something like that," agreed Stephanie.

"Did you have any luck getting enough physical evidence to tell who is telling the truth?" I asked.

Stephanie said, "Not yet. But there's still a lot of evidence to go through. So far nothing supports either of their statements one way or the other. But they are both party to the offences. How it rolls out in court depends on how the lawyers interpret things. Their defence will probably point fingers just as Angelo and Sophie are doing right now. Each swears to be the victim."

I knew Stephanie's team was still going through piles of evidence in an attempt to figure out who was the guilty party, or at least who was the *guiltiest* party. In my mind, they both seemed like monsters.

"This case could be a difficult case to prosecute if the two of them keep battling each other," Stephanie said. "Unless the prosecutor turns one of them against the other, it could take years until it gets to court." Then she paused and looked long and hard at me. "You seem different," she said. "How are you doing? You scared me when you hit the floor the other day."

I thought about lying again but decided I owed her the truth. I sighed. "The ticker's not so good," I admitted "I might have to get a bypass. I'm sorry for not telling you before."

Tears sprang to her eyes and she quickly looked away. "Alex, you should have told me sooner!" she said. She was mad but also sad, and she was trying not to cry. "I know we haven't been in touch, but you're special to me and I don't want to think that you're in danger. You've always been there for me … as a mentor, a co-worker and a friend. What can I do to help?"

"Aw, thanks, honey," I said softly. "But there is nothing you can do. It's up to the surgeons, my heart and the big guy upstairs."

She looked at me long and hard and said, "Alex, you're one of the nicest men I've ever met. As a cop, I know you gave everything you could to the job and you're one of the few people I know who really *loved* being a cop."

"Thanks, Stephanie," I said, touched.

"And I meant what I said," she said, eyeing me appraisingly. "If there is anything at all that I can do for you, or Karen, please call me." Then she grabbed both my arms, looked up and stared into my eyes. "You promise me that you will fight this and not give up," she said in a stern voice. "You are one of my star witnesses and you will not miss court, do you understand?"

I said, "Yes," and tears started to build in my eyes. It was my turn to look away.

I told her I had to go and we hugged and kissed each other on the cheek. Tears were rolling freely from the corners of her eyes now, and I had a tough time not crying myself. I told her I would stay in touch.

"I really care about you, Alex," she said.

"You're a very special friend," I said softly, and then I left.

After that conversation, suddenly I started to really realize how serious my heart condition was. I knew I had to drive over to Allan Featherstone's and end the trash man gig, so I got in my truck and went. When I got there, I met Allan in the employee locker room and he helped me clean out my locker. There wasn't much to do; I only had a couple of dirty shirts and a few pairs of pants stashed in there. I packed them up and then I walked to the lunchroom with Allan. Inside the lunch room, boy was I surprised. Allan had gathered up some of the office staff and drivers. He had cooler full of beer, some wine and a large tray of chicken wings. It was a nice surprise even though I hardly knew anyone, as they were day employees and I had worked the night shift.

I didn't tell Allan about my heart condition, but after a few beers I told him that if I didn't enjoy my second retirement I might consider coming back for the odd shift when he was short-staffed. "Great, give me a call anytime," he said.

It was a nice get-together. Allan and I told a few police war stories about the good old days, before cell phones and computers, to the amusement of Allan's workers. "Back then," we reminisced, "There were ashtrays on the desk, cigarettes being smoked in the office and carbon paper in the typewriters." How things have changed! I can remember when computers were *invented*, but most of the kids in that room never knew a time before them.

After the party, Allan wanted to go to a bar for some more drinks, but I said 'no' and told him I was on medication and couldn't mix it with alcohol. He asked me what medication and I just said 'antibiotics' and made up a story about having an infected toe from stepping on a nail. It was easier than talking about my heart. The truth was, I wanted to get home before Karen. She would be pissed to find out I was drinking and eating chicken wings when I was supposed to be doing things that were good for my heart.

When I got home, I threw some fish in the oven and then decided to check out my heart specialist, Dr. Jim Burns, on the

Internet. The Internet said he worked out of the Bisson City General Hospital—no surprise there—and that he was 40 years old. There was also a picture of his pretty wife and a bit of information about their four children.

I decided to give his office a call and see when I could get an appointment and I was pleasantly surprised to find out there was an opening the next day. The receptionist told me not to eat anything after midnight and to only drink water in the morning. Then she said she'd see me at 10:00 a.m.

I finished making dinner, and when Karen got home, I told her about the doctor's appointment. Then we had dinner and watched some television. She knew I had been drinking with Allan, but was glad I was going for the tests in the morning. I went to bed at 9:45, which is late for me, but I tossed and turned most of the night. I was actually pretty worried about my heart.

The next morning I was up around 5:00 a.m., missing my cup of coffee. By 7:00 a.m., when I usually eat, I was cranky and by 9:00 a.m., I was starving. Warm water wasn't cutting it. I drove to the hospital and went to Dr. Burns' office. The receptionist said I would need several different examinations, all in different rooms, and then I would give a fasting blood sample. When all that was done, then I would meet with Dr. Burns.

There was a pretty large group of us heart patients there that day and we followed each other through the different examination areas like cattle. There were little waiting areas with chairs outside each room and we chatted with each other as we waited. They checked my blood pressure, height, weight … the works. And then they took blood samples, as they'd promised.

In the X-ray area, I was told to undress and put on a hospital gown, and then I had a chest X-ray taken. After a few more examinations that I didn't understand, I was told to get dressed and go back to the main office. It wasn't too difficult to find my way back; they had little yellow stickers of feet on the floor to show me the way.

Back in the waiting area, I thought, *wow, foot stickers on the floor and a name tag … I feel like a little kid again.* It was probably a good idea, though, because there were a lot of elderly people going through the tests alongside me, and some of them seemed pretty confused.

I didn't have to wait too long before the receptionist called my name and I was escorted into Dr. Burns' office. Inside the office, I found all the diplomas on the wall I'd seen on my last visit to be quite reassuring. Today I also noticed some nice pictures of marine life and a fish tank that I hadn't seen before. It was very relaxing sitting in his office looking at those things. I wondered if he was into scuba diving or something. Then I wondered how many times Dr. Burns had to give life-shattering news to his patients.

Giving bad news is never easy. In that way, I knew I had something in common with the doctor. At times cops have to notify people that a loved one has somehow met a tragic end, and it is one of the most difficult things to do. You get used to it over time; it becomes part of the job. We also ensure they get some sort of support, from family members or a helping agency, to help them through the shock. I'm sure it's the same with doctors; I'm sure they develop nerves of steel over time. It's got to be hard to deliver bad news about medical conditions. But patients deserve to hear the truth, no matter how hard it is.

Dr. Burns entered the office. I stood up and shook his hand. He sat down behind his desk, opened a file folder, scanned the contents and then lowered his glasses and looked over the rims at me. He spoke in friendly manner but delivered the news I feared. "Alex," he said, "Your test results indicate that you need surgery right away, as early as next week if we can schedule it."

I didn't know what to say, so I just looked at him.

"I've done hundreds of surgeries like this and the chances are you'll make a full recovery. But you have two blocked coronary arteries. One is just about totally blocked so we'll have to graft a new artery around the blockage. The other is also blocked, but we couldn't determine to what the degree."

"Sounds serious," I said, swallowing my fear.

"It is, but it's treatable," Dr. Burns said. "Let me explain: When arteries get too narrow or blocked, it interferes with the heart muscle doing its job, which is pumping blood. Do you understand?"

I said, "Yes," and he nodded at me.

Then he asked, "Do you want to know about the actual process?"

Again I said, "Yes."

He said, "You will be given a general anesthesia and will fall asleep. I will make an eight- to ten-inch incision in your chest, going through your breast bone to expose the heart. A heart-lung bypass machine will keep your heart going while I work on the arteries. A grafted artery will be used to make a new path around the blocked artery, then I'll fix your breast bone, which will heal with time. After surgery, there will be two or three tubes in your chest to assist with drainage and you will have an intravenous drip as well. You'll be in intensive care for one night and then you'll have three to four days of recovery in a regular room."

"That doesn't sound too bad," I said weakly. I was lying; it sounded awful.

He acted like he never heard me. He continued, "There will be follow-up instruction on incision care, pain management, and rest and rehabilitation. And there will be at least six weeks of recovery before you start to feel better, though you might start feeling some benefits, like easier breathing, right away."

"Are there any risks associated with this heart surgery?" I asked.

"There are risks with any surgery," he said. "And just the fact that the surgeons are working on your arteries and heart is risky. But most people make a full recovery. Sometimes surgeons come across other issues during surgery, and if we do, we deal with it during the surgery. For example, if we open you up and find a third blocked artery, we would take a blood vessel from another part of your body and fix that too."

Just then, Dr. Burns got a phone call. He excused himself and he told me he had to see his receptionist. He returned a few minutes later with a handful of papers for me to sign.

"We had another cancellation, so I advise you to take this appointment, Alex," was all he said. Before I knew it, I was scheduled for surgery in a week. I couldn't believe they had all these cancellations. *My higher power must really want me to get this operation,* I thought.

It was nearly three-thirty in the afternoon when I left the hospital and northbound traffic was really heavy. Hearing what the doctor had to say stood out as one of the very few times in my life I've felt truly scared. The dialogue in my head started to talk me out of getting cut open. It said, *you've been feeling better lately do you really need the surgery?*

I shook my head at myself. "Grow up, Alex," I said out loud. I thought about Kobe, how bravely he'd faced surgery on his nose cancer, how scared he'd been at the vet's and how dopy he'd been after the anesthetic.

"Well, Kobe, old boy. I guess if you can get operated on, I can too," I said as I pulled into my driveway.

CHAPTER 7

I had to tell Karen that the surgery was next week and I also had to tell the kids about my health issues, probably this weekend.

Karen and I had done up a will years ago. If anything happened to me, Karen would get everything, including half my pension. I was sure she would be okay financially if I died; I had some money in the bank and had also secretly hidden a little cash in the house in case of emergencies. I didn't want to die, but I like to be prepared.

When Karen got home, she walked in, greeted me and asked, "What's for dinner?"

I said, "I'm not hungry. Listen, honey, you better sit down, I have some bad news." She sat on the sofa in the living room and I sat next to her. "I'm getting bypass surgery next week," I said, straight and to the point. "I have two blocked arteries and if I don't get the surgery, I'm going to die."

She was stunned. "You should have called me right after your doctor's appointment," she said, clearly upset and surprised at how fast surgery had been scheduled. However, she understood the need and ultimately was relieved that I decided to do something about it. "We'll get the kids over this weekend so we can tell them what's going on," she said.

After that, I was exhausted, so I went to bed early. I tossed and turned all night long and I think it was also a difficult night for Karen. I heard her on the phone before she went to bed, probably talking to one of her friends about the surgery. She needed some support.

I woke up with mixed feelings about the surgery and the possibility of dying. I thought, *what a way to enjoy your first day of real retirement.* No more trash man job.

I got up and had a coffee with Karen and then I watched the news while she got ready for work. She walked by me several times and I thought, *after all these years, she is still a beautiful woman with a great body.* She had kept herself in good shape and yes, she has a great ass.

Karen kissed me good bye and told me she had spoken to the kids and that both of them were coming home for the weekend. We discussed how we should break the news to them. She reminded me to take some time to go over all the paperwork I had received from Dr. Burns.

I was still scared about the surgery. I knew I had to have it, but it seemed like such a life and death situation. There were no guarantees that the surgery would be successful, though it sounded likely that it would. But what if it wasn't?

I'm ready to go, if I have to, I thought. I'd had a pretty good life. I'd worked at a job I enjoyed for over 30 years, exploring every area of policing I'd ever wanted to. I was promoted twice and retired at the rank of staff sergeant. I worked with many great law enforcement personnel over the years and I still have numerous friends on the force. But meeting and marrying Karen was the best thing that ever happened to me; watching our kids be born was indescribable and unforgettable; and, in general, being a parent made me a better man. Karen and I raised two beautiful children who turned into wonderful adults. We prepared them the best we could for their own life journeys and I'm positive each of them will have many great life experiences—jobs, marriages, and maybe even children. I want to be around to meet my grandchildren. I have to get this operation and I have to live.

With nothing planned for the whole day, I decided to go to

the bank and make sure everything would be financially okay for three or four months while I recovered. After that, I decided to draft some letters for Karen and the kids in case I didn't make it. I wanted them to understand how I felt about them and how grateful I was to have been able to share my life with them.

When I got back from the bank, I went on the Internet and checked for updates on the homicide investigation. There were numerous stories and police had finally released the names of the accused and some pictures. The media had researched Sophie and Angelo Martino as best they could by interviewing various neighbors or anyone they could find who'd frequented the hot dog cart. Reports portrayed them as alcoholic murderers who were barely making a living and were constantly arguing and fighting. There were no details from the prosecutor's office yet about the nature of the case against them, though.

I decided I had to get out of the house for a while, so I went for a walk. As I walked slowly through the subdivision, I really missed Kobe. I didn't have any chest pains or anything, but I thought, *this could be the last time I get to do this. Maybe I'll see you soon, Kobe old boy.* It gave me new eyes, and I looked closely at everything—the houses, the trees and the roads. I was starting to realize how precious life really is. I wasn't in pain and I felt pretty good. *The medication is doing its job.*

When I got home, I went through the medical package from Dr. Burns again. It contained information on what I had to do prior to surgery, what time I had to report and prep, and what time they would cut me open. I was still surprised about the quick surgery date, and a little worried because, though I had lost *some* weight, I wasn't sure it was as much as I should have. I was nervous as hell. In my life, I've generally been pretty healthy and not had to see a doctor very often, so this was a big deal to me. Until now, the only surgery I'd ever had was for a few broken fingers when I was a kid and a hernia when I was in my 30s. Neither are comparable to heart surgery.

When Karen came home she said, "It's all arranged. The kids will be here this weekend. Oh, and Alex? I'm taking time off to be with you before and after the surgery. I'm going to make sure you get through this."

I was grateful. I hugged her.

We hadn't seen the kids for a couple of months, and so when Chloe and Jamie came home on Friday night, I was happy to see them, even if the circumstances were not ideal. Jamie noticed right away that something wasn't right. "Hi, Dad," he said, hugging me tightly. Then he pulled away and said, "You look kind of grey. Are you okay?"

I just nodded. Explanations could wait.

That night we had a nice family dinner and I teased Jamie about becoming a police officer. I have never pushed either of them into law enforcement, but I silently hoped one of them would consider it as a career. However, mostly I hoped whatever they chose was something they were happy doing. That seemed to be the case so far. Jamie still loved his job in Kingston, and Chloe was happy at school and had been dating the same guy for over two years.

We didn't break the news until the next morning. When we told them, both kids were surprised and asked a lot of questions, which I answered as best I could.

"I wanted you to know what was going on," I told them, "But I don't want you to worry. You need to stay at your school and work and continue to create your lives. Your mom will be with me and she will keep you updated on what's going on."

On Sunday, both kids wished me good luck, hugged me, said good bye and left. I was sad to see them go and also wondered if it would be the last time I would ever see them. I gave them both extra-big hugs. I was able to convince *them* that the surgery wasn't that dangerous, but I still hadn't been able to convince *myself.*

Karen and I rattled around in the house after they left and I found it odd how we seemed to seek each other out in a way we hadn't for a while. It's strange how, when you spend so many years with your spouse, sometimes the intimacy drifts away from the relationship, even though you're still there for one another. For the first time in years, Karen seemed to be extra close to me. I guess sometimes a family crisis causes people to become closer. Neither of us had experienced anything like this before and so that night we held hands and cuddled. It was nice to feel her body against mine. Her skin was so soft, and her touch felt so nice. We made love like we hadn't done in a long time, not rushed, just slow and loving. Maybe we were both thinking this could be the last time we might ever be intimate. I realized how, even after the kids moved out, we'd been too busy to rekindle our love and love-making. I wish we'd communicated with each other better and done this more often.

I spent the next few days feeling introspective about life. *Did I enjoy life to its fullest? Did I do everything I wanted to do and accomplish? Will I be remembered as a good person? A good father and husband?*

On Wednesday night I followed all the instructions in the folder and Karen helped me pack a hospital bag. That night, when I lay in bed next to Karen, I told her I was very lucky to have met her. I said, "I didn't say 'I love you' as much as I should have. If I get better, we should enjoy life more and go on some trips."

Karen stopped me. "It's not *if*, Alex. It's *when*. And I love you too. Now get some sleep."

We got up early and drove to the hospital. When we go to the reception area, the nurse told Karen she would have to wait in the waiting room. I hugged Karen good bye and told her I loved her. Then I said, "Thank you."

She said, "I love you too ... and why are you saying thank you?"

"For being my wife and the mother of our beautiful children," I told her. Then, as I walked away, I wondered if that would be the last time I would ever see her.

I followed the nurse's instructions to undress and put on a small, drafty hospital gown. Then I lay down on the stretcher. Soon, I was pushed through a number of hallways and ended up in the operating room, where a group of doctors and nurses waited for me. I heard a voice say, "Alex, I'm going to put this mask on you and the gas will make you go to sleep. Start counting backwards from 100." All I remember after that was that the operating room had a lot of lights on the ceiling.

It seemed like only minutes before I opened my eyes again. I didn't know where I was. I tried to focus and figure it out, but it was difficult because I felt so groggy. I tried to move my arm and found that I was as stiff as a board and felt like I had been hit by a truck. Then I realized I was in a hospital room. Suddenly I remembered why I was there. I didn't remember anything about the surgery, and now the whole thing was over. It was weird.

A nurse was standing next to me. "How do you feel?" she asked.

I told her, "I feel dizzy and little out of it."

She said, "Things will become clearer in a few minutes. Your wife is in the waiting room down the hall. As soon as I clean you up a bit, when you're ready, she would like to come and see you."

About an hour later, I felt a little better and the nurse brought Karen into my room. She rushed in and kissed me on the forehead. She asked, How are you feeling?"

I said, "Okay, I think."

Karen said, "Everybody is outside in the waiting room. They all want to know how you're doing."

I said, "Who's everybody?"

She said, "The kids, Stephanie, Corey and some people I've never met before. There's some old guy named Joe out there too. He smells a little."

I asked, "How did they know I was having heart surgery?"

She said, "Stephanie tried to get hold of you, and when you

didn't answer she called me, and I told her. Stephanie must have told the others."

After a few minutes, the nurse said I needed to rest for the next 24 hours and that I couldn't have any visitors for a while. I asked if I could see the kids for a few minutes and she said 'yes'.

"Thank everyone who showed up," I told Karen. "Tell them I'll speak to them soon." She nodded.

The kids came in and asked how I was doing. They looked pretty upset at seeing me in a hospital bed. I said I was okay and thanked them for coming. Then I told them I was really tired. They hugged me and left and I drifted back to sleep.

During the next couple of days, I slowly had most of the tubes removed and was allowed to have a few visitors. Karen came by every day and Stephanie and Corey stopped by too. Karen and the kids got me some flowers, which cheered up the room. I thought that a shot of whiskey might also help my recovery, but no one brought me any.

The first time Stephanie and Corey stopped by, I was too tired to talk much, but I perked up by the second time and asked them about the investigation and how was it going.

"We searched their house and found evidence suggesting someone had been held in chains in the basement," Stephanie told me. "There was a chain with handcuffs attached to a post and whoever it was might have been in that basement for a while. There was also a small bed and clothes scattered about. Forensics ripped the place apart looking for evidence, but so far the only DNA they found matches Sophie and Angelo Martino. It was Sophie's DNA on the handcuffs. Angelo's was found in and around the bed."

"Interesting," I said.

"Sure is," said Corey, adding, "We re-interviewed Sophie specifically about the chain and handcuffs and she made a very self-serving statement indicating that Angelo used to chain her up in the basement when she did something wrong or when she complained about having to help him with the killings. She said he'd beat her and rape her until he broke her will and then she would reluctantly help him again."

Stephanie added, "We gave the new evidence to the prosecutor's office. They're negotiating a plea bargain with Sophie's attorney. They're considering turning her into a witness for the prosecution, providing she pleads guilty to 'accessory after the fact' on all seven charges. If that's how it unrolls, Sophie might get seven years and be eligible for parole in three."

"So it would seem it's Sophie's version of events that is holding up," I commented.

"Yup," said Stephanie.

"She didn't seem like much of a victim to me," I said, angry at the thought of Sophie being portrayed as such. I then heard my heart-monitor start beeping faster and decided I better settle down. I sighed. "Obviously you know the case a lot better than me, but I think you're making a deal with the devil."

Corey shrugged. "At least they're both going to jail. That's a win."

"Do you support the prosecutor's decision?" I asked Stephanie. "Is it not possible that Sophie could have been the dominant aggressor, controlling Angelo? In my opinion, they were *both* party to the offence and they should be charged jointly."

"Well, nothing is finalized yet, Alex," said Stephanie. "My team will have further meetings with the prosecution, but I know the prosecutor thinks they have the strongest case if they use Sophie against Angelo. It's not the ideal solution to charge them jointly and running one trial ... but it would be too costly to run two separate trials."

"I know," I said, "But there is something evil about that woman. I know she's as guilty as he is. I guess it won't go to trial for about a year, though, right?"

Stephanie nodded. "And you'll be testifying as a witness at the beginning of the trial," she said. She added, "We expect Angelo to plead not guilty."

Then Stephanie kissed me on the forehead and Corey shook my hand and they both told me, "Get better!" and left.

CHAPTER 8

It was my fourth day in the hospital and I was feeling better, though my chest felt sore and I'd lost about twenty pounds.

I was thinking, *enough with the ice water, Jell-O, mashed potatoes and beans.* It would be so nice to have a steak with a little blue cheese and mushrooms on it, as well as a cold beer. I was looking forward to going home.

Once I got home, my bandages would have to be changed every day to prevent infection and I'd have to take sponge baths until my wound was well enough that I could shower. *Maybe Karen will give me a special sponge bath when I get home,* I mused. That's when I knew for sure I was feeling better.

In terms of ongoing care, Karen was taking time off and after that she planned to check on me every day on her lunch breaks. As I thought about Karen, she suddenly walked into my room. She looked so pretty and was wearing a nice dress and a short jacket; very professional. She was dressed for the business world. She greeted me with a kiss.

"Hi Alex," she said, "I came by early, as Dr. Burns is supposed to stop by with the results of your surgery and I wanted to hear what he had to say."

"I hope he sends me home," I said. "I'm still pretty weak and sore, but I think I could survive okay at home." However I still had a catheter in me and I had to have assistance walking to the bathroom for a crap.

About fifteen minutes later, Dr. Burns showed up. He had my chart with him and asked me how I was. I said, "I feel like I was hit by a truck, but I'm still here and happy to be alive."

He said hello to Karen and shook her hand. "He's a fighter, your husband," he told her, as if I wasn't there. "He'll be home in a couple of days and a nurse will do home visits once a day for the next two weeks. She'll change the bandage and assist and guide you both."

Then he looked at me and said, "Alex, I have good news and bad news for you. We discovered blockages in *four* of the main arteries to your heart and we ended up doing a triple by-pass instead of a double. But we couldn't do the fourth artery because we didn't have enough time. It's just about totally blocked and, though some blood is still getting through, the blockage could lead to another heart attack or a stroke, which is, of course, not great news. The good news is that with the assistance of medication and some lifestyle you should be able to live at least another ten years. Some people live a healthy life with one blocked artery."

Karen looked pained. I could tell she wanted better news.

The doctor noted her expression and added, "This is not a death sentence. You will have a great quality of life and, as I said, some people live a very long time with this condition. But you will need regular checkups to ensure your heart and blood pressure are closely monitored, and if you have any chest pains, you need to get to the hospital right away."

Karen and I looked at each other. The news was not what we were hoping for. I said to her, "Oh well, not the greatest news ... but it sounds like you are stuck with me for at least another ten years."

"That's not so bad," she said, giving me a hug.

"The key is to eat healthily, exercise moderately and enjoy your life," said Dr. Burns. "Avoid stressful situations ... and I want to see you monthly. If you have any issues, surgery is always an option. But we're going to have to let that go until you get back on your feet and discover how you feel."

He left after he delivered the news and after a while Karen went back to work too. I lay in the hospital bed, looking out the window. Then I heard a noise at the door and looked up to see Old Joe, or Steam Pipe Joe as some people call him. He said, "Hi, Alex. How are you doing?"

I said, "Not bad. Come in and have a seat."

Joe pulled up a chair and sat next to the bed. Karen was right; he did have a certain smell attached to him.

"I've been trying to get in to see you for a couple of days," he said, "But the hospital security staff escorted me out every time."

"Sorry, Joe. Some people are close-minded and if someone looks different, they treat them differently, too, I guess," I said. Then I asked, "Are you ready for winter? I've noticed the nights getting chilly."

"Yes," he said. "I live on the steam pipe as long as possible, but in January and February I go into a shelter."

"That's good thinking," I said. Then I told him I was going to be released soon. "Finally I can get out of this place and go home. Hospitals are the worst."

"Are you going to be driving the garbage truck anymore?" Joe asked.

I said, "I'm not sure. Maybe in a few months, when I feel better."

"The girls downtown miss you," he told me. Then he asked me, "Did you know I'm going to be a witness in court against the Martinos?"

"Me too," I said.

"I'm kind of scared to go to court," he said.

"Me too," I said again. Then I added, "It might not take all that long for it to get to court. It sounds like Sophie Martino might get a deal to testify against her husband. According to her, he regularly beat the crap out of her."

Joe started shaking his head. He said, "No, Alex, that's not right."

I asked, "What do you mean, Joe?"

He said, "Over the last three or four years I've seen them working together many times and it's always Sophie yelling at Angelo, giving him orders and telling him he's no good. I've even seen her swat him on the back of the head with a wooden spoon."

"Did you tell the police that?" I asked him.

"No, they never asked me anything about that stuff," he said. "They only wanted to know what I saw the night they dumped that girl in the river."

I told him, "It's important that you tell them, Joe. Make sure you tell Stephanie and Corey what you saw. I'm going to get them to speak with you again."

"Okay," he said.

I told him it was nice to see him, and thanked him for coming.

"Get better," he said and then he left.

I was released from the hospital on a Thursday, exactly a week after I went in for surgery. The ride home exhausted me. Sitting up in the front passenger seat was a challenge and it made my chest ache. Karen was driving, and she kept wincing on my behalf every time we went over a bump.

It was nice to get home. I had only been in hospital about a week, but it was long enough. Soon I settled into a routine. The nurse came every day for the first week and then every second day the following week. A personal service worker came to the house a couple of times a week to give me a sponge bath and make sure I had enough to eat and drink. They were nice, but I got no hot nurses out of the deal. A couple of times it was even a *male* nurse who sponged me. Karen laughed when I told her that. "Gender doesn't matter as long as they do their jobs," she said.

Soon Karen returned to her regular shifts. I was much better but still trying to heal so I took it easy and I even wound up losing about 20 pounds, even though I mostly spent my time watching television. Sometimes I got on the laptop and surfed the web, but I avoided reading about the murders.

Time passed quickly and before I knew it, winter arrived followed by Christmas. By now I was up and about and feeling pretty good. I was strong enough to go to the gym again and was able to do some light cardio workouts. I had to watch what I was eating, though, and I cut my drinking down quite a bit.

The kids came home for the holidays and we had a nice Christmas with them and other assorted family members. All in all, I was feeling pretty good, pretty lucky and at peace with my situation.

After the holidays, in January, I got a call from Stephanie. We hadn't spoken since she and Corey had visited me in the hospital. "You're sounding good, Alex," she said. "It's nice to hear your voice back to it's usual level."

"Thanks, Stephanie," I said.

"How do you feel about lunch?" she asked. "I can update you on the investigation and trial. I have to subpoena you. It starts in July."

"Well, I'd like to see you but I'm not comfortable or strong enough to drive to Bisson City yet," I said.

"No problem," she said. "We can meet you tomorrow for lunch at that wing restaurant near your house."

"Great, I'll have a salad," I said. She laughed.

I spent the afternoon on the Internet catching up on the murders. The media had published a lot of information about the victims and their families. Sadly, the seventh victim, Jane Doe, had not been properly identified yet. Stories about the Martinos portrayed Sophie as an abused victim of domestic violence. Female activists and support groups were lining up to support 'poor' victimized Sophie. I shook my head in disgust. I fully understand domestic violence and firmly believe victims of domestic violence need community support and that their abusers should be held accountable in a court of law. However, I didn't believe Sophie was a victim. She was far too confident and shrewd to let anyone abuse her.

I was pretty engrossed in the stories I was reading and all of a sudden I heard Karen walking in the door. I shut off the computer and quickly said, "I'm taking you out for dinner!" We went to a nearby restaurant for salads.

During dinner I told Karen that Stephanie and Corey were taking me out for lunch tomorrow and that they had to serve me a subpoena. Karen was a little concerned. "Will the stress of going to court bother you?" she asked.

"It doesn't start until July. I should be fine by then," I told her.

The next day I went to the restaurant to meet Stephanie and Corey for lunch. When I walked in, I was pleased to see Stephanie was alone. I liked Corey, but I didn't know him that well yet and I sometimes felt like he thought I was a foolish old coot, though I knew he appreciated my advice.

Stephanie got up from the table and hugged me. I asked her where Corey was and she said, "He's busy in the office and he didn't want to drive this far." The waitress came by and I ordered a couple of drinks. Stephanie looked at me and said, "Alex, are you allowed drink?"

I said, "The odd one is okay," and then I said, "I guess I really shouldn't order chicken wings, either." I glanced at Stephanie and in the light of the window we were sitting beside, I noticed she looked tired and appeared to have lost some weight. I asked her, "Is everything okay?"

She said, "The publicity about the murders is compromising the trial. Somehow, the media is accessing information they shouldn't have, personal information about both the killers and the victims."

"Do you have a leak?" I asked.

"I don't know yet," she admitted. "I don't think so."

"You better find out," I said, "This is the biggest murder

investigation Bisson City has ever seen. You want to put these guys away."

"I know," she said.

"You have to expect some problems. There are no perfect homicide investigations. Deal with this hurdle and move on." She nodded glumly. I could tell she was beat. "You're in it for the long haul. You know that," I said gently. "Pace yourself, eat properly, exercise and get enough sleep. And even though you're thinking about the investigation the minute you get out of bed, take time off and try to enjoy other things. Being a cop is only one part of life. Believe me, I know. Manage the stress and pressure like you do everything else."

"You're right, the investigation is taking its toll and I need to watch it or I'm going to wind up like you, with a triple bypass."

"You bet your sweet ass you will," I said, happily munching on the veggie sticks I'd ordered instead of fries.

As we ate lunch, she updated me on the investigation. Jane Doe had finally been identified as 18-year-old Mary St. Cyr from Montreal. Mary's parents had reported her missing about a year ago. They told police they had raised their three children as strict Catholics but Mary, being a teenage girl who didn't like the strict rules, had run away."

"The classic tale," I said wryly. Then I asked, "Did your team have a chance to re-interview Old Joe? He had some interesting things to say about Sophie and Angelo fighting with each other."

Stephanie said, "Corey interviewed him and Joe told him about what he had seen and heard, but he couldn't remember any specifics, like dates, locations and time. For us to prove Sophie beat Angelo, we need substantive details. But still, his statement was interesting. It provided substance to the idea that Sophie was the aggressor and leader. But without corroborating evidence, it would be difficult to prove it in court."

"That's frustrating," I said. "I just know that woman is a witch."

Stephanie laughed. Then she asked, "How are you feeling these days?"

"Physically, I'm on the mend," I told her, "But at times I'm a little bored with the hard job of taking it easy. I was thinking about calling Featherstone's and maybe doing one shift a week."

She said, "You're crazy. You should take it easy and enjoy your retirement, Alex."

"Until Karen retires too, it's going to be pretty boring. There are only so many times a week you can go to the gym, and only so many odd jobs around the house to do. I'm just looking for one or two days a week to keep me engaged," I said.

"You sure don't like to sit still," she told me. "Oh, and by the way, I have a witness subpoena for you. They elected to bypass the preliminary hearing and go directly to trial against Angelo. Seven counts of first-degree murder."

I asked, "What's going on with Sophie?"

"You won't be happy about this," she said. "After numerous meetings with the prosecutor, and a close review of all the evidence, the prosecutor decided to accept a guilty plea for seven counts of accessary to murder after the fact. Then they'll use her as a witness against Angelo."

I said, "You're right, that pisses me off. I still say it's a deal with the devil and they should charge them jointly with all the murders."

"Sorry, it's a done deal," said Stephanie. "Sophie will plead out in early June and the trial will follow in July. There are indications that there will be lots of legal arguments between the defence attorney and the prosecutor, so that might even delay things into August, since the trial won't actually start until the legal arguments are complete."

Still fuming over what Stephanie had said, I ordered us another drink. She excused herself and went to the washroom. As usual I checked out her butt as she walked away and I could really see how much weight she'd lost, because her usually very tight, form-fitting pants were a little baggy.

When she returned, she said, "Okay, Alex, this is the last drink for me as I have to get back to the office."

"Sure," I said. Then I added, "I noticed when you walked away that you've lost some weight."

Stephanie smiled. "I saw you in the mirror checking out my ass while I was walking away."

I said, "What I can say? You caught me." Then I said seriously, "Look after yourself, okay? You didn't have any weight to lose in the first place, so don't lose any more."

We finished our lunch and walked outside to the parking lot. Stephanie picked up the tab, saying, "This is a work-related lunch."

As we hugged each other and said good bye, she grabbed my hand and stuck it on her butt. She said, "Hey Alex, I think your eyesight is failing. What do you think?"

Her butt felt very firm and I said, "You're right, I guess. I should get glasses."

We laughed together and she said she would be in touch with me regarding court.

As she got in her car and drove away, I tried to remember how old Stephanie was. I guessed she was about 40. *Sure enough, that makes me just old enough to be her father,* I thought.

When I got home I noticed my shirt had the smell of Stephanie's perfume on it. It wasn't a big deal, but I didn't want Karen to get the wrong idea, so I took off my shirt and ran it through the washing machine with some other laundry. Then, as I walked by the mirror with no shirt on, I examined the large scar from the surgery. It ran down my chest from my heart to about six inches above my belly button. *My body has certainly changed,* I thought. I was working out on a daily basis and had lost nearly 25 pounds, but instead of a six-pack abdomen I had a saggy nine-pack. There was extra skin hanging from a few places—possibly from the weight loss. Worse, my balls seemed to be sagging more and more as well. There are little hairs starting to grow in strange places, like my ears and I have to get my eyebrows trimmed every time I get a haircut. But worst of all is that I now have to get up two or three times a night to piss.

I started feeling a little depressed, so I quickly put my shirt back on and started making dinner for Karen. When Karen got home, she walked in and immediately saw the subpoena lying on the kitchen counter. She looked at it quickly and asked, "How was lunch with Corey and Stephanie?"

I said, "Okay, but Corey couldn't make it so it was just Stephanie and me. It was good and Stephanie updated me on the investigation. But that kid works too hard. She looks burnt out and has lost weight."

"So what did you have for lunch?" Karen asked suspiciously.

I said, "Yeah, I know. I had couple of draft beers and wings. But I passed on the fries and had veggie sticks instead." Karen just shook her head and walked away.

We had dinner together and then Karen went out shopping for a few hours, so I started surfing the Internet, looking for more information on the murders. In the back of my mind, I was still pissed off about the deal Sophie was getting, and when I started looking at pictures of the seven victims, I got even madder. I thought, *they were so young and pretty. Their poor parents.*

Then for some unknown reason, I started sweating and suddenly felt a pain in my arm. I thought, *oh no is this happening again?* I had already taken my daily medication, so I ran to the kitchen and popped some aspirin into my mouth. Then I sat on the couch in the living room for a while.

I must have passed out, because I came to when I heard Karen remotely opening the garage door. I sat up and put the television on just as she walked in. Karen took one look at me and asked, "Are you okay?"

I lied and said, "Yes."

She saw the open aspirin container on the kitchen counter. "What's going on, Alex?" she asked.

I said, "I don't know. The two beers I had may have affected my medication. I'm not feeling one hundred percent, so I took some aspirin."

"Alex you be careful," she said, clearly worried.

"Okay," I replied, and I realized this was probably not a good time to talk to her about the court case or about going back to work at Featherstone's. *Maybe it was a pulled muscle or something,* I thought. Soon I forgot about it.

As summer approached, I started pleading with Karen about working at Featherstone's again. She finally gave in and said it was okay with her if I returned to work on Sunday nights only. "One eight-hour shift a week, and that's it," she said. I was happy with that. I hadn't had any more chest pains, and I'd lost more weight, which was good.

I worked my one day a week through June and into the beginning of July. The job was still easy; nothing had changed. First the cardboard run, then the garbage run. I could almost do it with my eyes closed. Nothing complicated there.

In the middle of July, I got a call from Stephanie. She said the legal arguments and jury selection were proceeding slowly and that I wouldn't have to testify until late August or early September. "I'll phone you about a week before you're expected to testify so you can attend a court preparation meeting with the prosecutor," she told me. Then we chatted for a few minutes and Stephanie said she had to get back to work. I started to think about testifying. I thought that after I was done, depending on my health, I wanted to watch portions of the trial.

There is a lot of work that goes into presenting and preparing evidence for a homicide trial, let alone a trial involving serial killers who have killed seven people. The police have to build an airtight case if they want to see killers go to jail, and that involves managing vast amounts of data. In Ontario, police and prosecutors use the Ontario Major Case Management (OMCM) system, a secure information management tool to manage large amounts of data.

There are three key players in any homicide investigation; the case manager, the primary investigator and the file coordinator who works the OMCM. When I was a homicide cop, I worked in all three positions at one time or another. I spent long hours assisting prosecutors with preparing evidence, both physical (i.e., a weapon or DNA) and witness-based. Physical evidence required precise chain-of-custody record-keeping to ensure evidence wasn't tampered with. Witness-based evidence involved obtaining written statements, often from people who are grieving or in shock. Sometimes I had to meet with the families of victims to help them understand the court process. It was hands-on work and emotionally draining to boot. I could imagine how hard it was for Stephanie's team to deal with the families of the Martinos' victims, and how much evidence the group must be painstakingly sorting through.

It must be overwhelming and exhausting, I thought, as I prepared for my Sunday night trash man shift. When I thought about that stress and how much strain I'd put on my heart over the years working in such an intense way, I was suddenly grateful to be out of it. *Kobe, old boy,* I thought as I climbed into my Featherstone's trash truck, *you may not be around to see my grandchildren, but I want to be.*

CHAPTER 9

I made it down to Featherstone's yard and parked my pickup truck. Working only one night shift a week meant that another night shift worker was using the truck the rest of the week. This person also left his garbage all over the cab and so lately I've had to spend the first ten minutes of my shift cleaning up his crap. It's annoying. How can a trash man be so trashy?

It reminded me of a when I was in uniform and driving marked police cruisers for 12-hour shifts. With that kind of schedule, your car becomes your office, your lunch room, and your personal space for 12 hours. It was inevitable that messes were made ... but most officers would gas up and clean up before booking off their shift. Some didn't though. I remember finding garbage left behind by one particular officer more than once. One day I gathered it all up in a bag and put it in his mailbox with a note. The note said, *I'm not your mother or your maid so clean up your garbage.* I didn't have any further issues with that officer.

I stopped and got coffee at Pete's. The hookers were out tonight as usual and of course they flirted and razzed me when I walked by them. However, tonight their energy was a little different. I think word must have gotten out that I assisted in the homicide investigation. Some of the girls who had once made fun of the trash man were now calling me Alex and talking to me in a different tone of voice, with more respect.

I got a coffee and was about to leave when I saw Old Joe

pushing his cart down the street. I hadn't seen him for a while. I quickly grabbed him a coffee and a couple of sandwiches and ran down the street after him, yelling at him to stop. He saw me and stopped right away. He was happy to see me and surprised that I was driving the truck again. He thanked me for the coffee and sandwiches.

"How are you feeling about court?" I asked him.

"I'm nervous and I feel like I really don't fit in with the type of people who will be in that courthouse," he said.

"Don't worry, Joe, we all get nervous going to court," I told him. "Just review your statement before you go in and if you are asked a question you don't know the answer to, be honest. Tell them you don't know the answer."

I reached into my pocket and found 60 dollars. I said, "Joe, here's some money to help you fit in better at court. Get a haircut, shave and shower. See if you can find a nice pair of pants and a shirt somewhere."

Joe just held the money in his hand, looking at it. Then he said, "Alex, you're a true gentleman. I know what you are trying to do, but I don't need your money. Don't worry about me. That Corey cop and the lady cop already spoke to me about court. They said the day before court someone will meet me and take me to get cleaned up."

Then he handed me the 60 dollars back. I pocketed 40 and made him take the other 20. I said, "No arguments, you keep this."

"Thanks," Joe said. Then he gave me a quick hug before he walked away, pushing his cart. I watched him and thought, *if people knew about the tragic loss of that man's family, they would treat him a lot differently.* He may struggle with mental health problems, and he may not be up on hygiene, but he is a good-hearted man.

I got back into the truck and did my run. There was a lot of cardboard and garbage in the various bins so I was busy. Around three-thirty in the morning, my cell phone rang, startling me. No one would call me at that time so I was worried that something was wrong with Karen. However, the phone number was blocked, so I knew it wasn't her.

"Hello?" I said.

Some guy asked, "Are you Alex?"

I said, 'yes' and he said his name was Ralph and that he owned Ralph's Bar and Grill over on Parliament Street. He said there was a drunken female named Stephanie passed out in his bar.

"She's so drunk she can't even stand up," he said, "I need her removed so I can close up. She gave me your number and told me to call you."

I had just emptied the truck at the dump, which was lucky, and I knew where Ralph's Bar was, so I said, "Okay. Just watch her and I'll be there in about 20 minutes. Then I drove the garbage truck over there as fast as I could. When I walked in, I asked the guy behind the bar, "Are you Ralph?"

"Yup. That Stephanie woman is in the washroom throwing up."

I went to the ladies' washroom and knocked on the door. I didn't get a response, so I walked in, calling Stephanie's name. There was still no response. I looked under the stall doors and saw a pair of legs splayed out on the floor right next to the toilet. I pushed the stall door open. What a mess. It looked like Stephanie had thrown up a couple of times. Her clothing was dishevelled and her hair, which was usually in some type of bun, was now hanging down, covering her face. She was completely passed out so I put my hand on her shoulder and shook her. She woke up.

"You're gonna be okay," I said as I helped her off the floor.

She started crying and said, "I'm sorry, I'm so sorry, I told him to call you."

"Don't worry about it," I said. "What are friends for?"

I took her to the sink and used wet paper towels to clean up her face, blouse and pants. She had been sick all over herself.

As I helped her out of the bar I stopped and gave Ralph 20 bucks. "Sorry about the mess in the washroom," I said.

"Yeah, thanks. But what do you expect from someone when they power drink for hours?"

My first thought was, *well who served her the booze?* But I kept my mouth shut and helped Stephanie out of the bar to my truck.

I poured her into the passenger side of the garbage truck and told her to hold the plastic bag I'd given her in case she had to throw up. "I don't know where you live," I said.

"Brent Street just north of Water Street," she told me.

As I drove her home, her head nodded back and forth and soon she was sleeping, leaning against the passenger side window for most of the ride home. I pulled the truck up to the visitors' parking area near her front door, taking up two and half parking spaces and then woke her up and helped her out of the truck. I asked for her keys and she dug them out of her pocket.

I wasn't sure if she'd started the evening with a purse; in all the time I'd known her, she'd kept most of her things in her pockets. I thought I better check. "Do you have a purse?" I asked.

She shook her head, side to side, 'no'. She was sloppy and giggling as we went into the building. She told me we had to take the elevator to the fourth floor, so I called it and we got in. Once inside, I propped her up in the corner. Her head was hanging down and her long hair was covering her face. I never realized she had all that hair. She muttered something about finally going to her place to get lucky.

I half-dragged, half-carried her down the hall, unlocked her condo and helped her inside. She kicked off her shoes and flopped on the couch. I looked around and admired how huge and beautiful her place was. I was impressed.

Stephanie started to snore, and I said, "You can't pass out there. You'll wreck your pretty couch." I pulled her to her feet. She was pretty groggy, so I walked her to the bigger of two bedrooms. It was a nice large bedroom, clearly feminine. I sat her down on the bed. She had puke stains on her top, and though I felt weird about it, I helped her get it off. She uttered something about me finally wanting to fuck her, and I said, "That's not it, my dear. I'm just trying not to throw up because of the smell from the vomit. You're covered in puke and I can't stand it."

Pulling her shirt off exposed a cute bra that contained surprisingly large breasts. She was way too drunk to notice if I stared or not, but I didn't. I didn't want to take advantage of a friend.

As soon as her shirt was off, she fell flat onto the bad and passed out. I looked at her and realized that her pants were also covered in puke, so I undid them and pulled them off too. Surprisingly, underneath she was wearing a tight pair of boxers with a Maple Leafs hockey emblem on them. *That's different*, I thought. I expected her to be more of a sexy thong girl.

I'm not gonna lie; I had a quick glance at her body because I'm only human, but then, after turning her onto her side in case she puked again, I grabbed a blanket and covered her up. Then I threw her dirty clothing into a bag, turned on a night light for her and got my coat. I was about to leave when I realized I couldn't lock her door without taking her keys with me.

"Aw, crap," I said. I decided I would lock her door, take the garbage truck back to the yard, grab my pickup truck and come back. I texted Karen to tell her I was running late and would miss our morning coffee.

I got back to Stephanie's about an hour later and let myself in. I checked on her and she was still soundly sleeping, snoring lightly. I went to the living room, sat on the couch and turned the television, with the volume set low. I started to fall asleep and then I heard a phone ringing. Stephanie answered and said something about needing a few hours off, and that she would be in to work later. Then I then fell asleep on the couch.

It didn't seem like long before I heard someone saying, "Alex, hey Alex … time to wake up."

I opened my eyes and saw Stephanie standing there in a robe. Her hair was wet and she smelled way better than she had when I put her to bed.

"What time was it?" I asked groggily.

"Around eleven," she told me.

I sat up and stretched.

"I made us some coffee and eggs," she said.

"Sounds good," I told her. "I just have to go to the washroom, and I'll be right there."

She was seated at the kitchen island nursing a coffee when I finished in the can. I asked her, "How are you feeling?"

"I feel terrible," she said, "I have a hangover plus I'm really embarrassed about getting the bar owner to call you."

"Hey, don't worry. Everyone gets a little sloppy once in a while," I told her.

She asked me, "What happened?"

I said, "You gave my phone number to Ralph and he called me to come and pick you up. I found you in the washroom throwing up. I cleaned you up a bit and drove you home. Then I escorted you into your condo and put you to bed."

She looked up from her coffee sheepishly and asked, "Did we do anything?"

I said, straight-faced, "Well, I didn't really want to do anything, but you grabbed me and pulled me into bed on top of you. It was beautiful and we had sex twice. At one point, you commented that I was *huge*. We went at it pretty good. You exhausted me. I was afraid you might throw up again, but you didn't. Then, when we were done, I put a garbage container next to you and came out here to the couch to sleep."

Stephanie looked sheepish. "I don't remember anything. But I don't *feel* like I had sex." I couldn't hold back anymore; I started laughing. She said, "Hey, what are you laughing at?"

"I was just joking, nothing had happened between us. But I want you to realize that anything could have happened to you at the bar, and as drunk as you were, you wouldn't have been able to stop it, or even remember it."

This was not news to her, but it sucked for her to hear it from me. Then I told her I had been almost a perfect gentleman, tucking her into bed. Stephanie said, "What does that mean? What does 'almost a perfect gentleman' mean?"

"I helped you out of your blouse and pants because you had puked all over yourself. I left your bra and panties on … but I had to take a few seconds to check out the goods before I put the covers on you."

"I see," she said. Then she laughed, walked around the counter, hugged me and said, "Thanks." As she hugged me, her robe opened, exposing one of her breasts. She said to me, "Do you want to check the goods out a bit better now?"

I did and I had to pause for a couple of seconds, thinking about her offer and the consequences. My libido shouted, 'yes, yes, yes,' as I thought about having sex with her, while my mind said, 'wife, bad heart, a whole life up in smoke.' I glanced down at her exposed breast again. It was large and nicely shaped. She had a nice nipple. Then, as much as I didn't want to, I said, "Sorry, I can't. The goods look amazing, but I can't touch them."

She stepped back and pulled her robe together and said, "Sorry, I don't know what's wrong with me. Then she said she had to go to the washroom and she walked away. As I watched her go, I realized that her robe was see-though and that it did not cover her, or her butt, very well. She had a nice-looking, firm butt with a little jiggle in it. I thought, *what a beautiful woman. Am I stupid to turn her down?* I knew I had hurt her feelings by doing so.

I grabbed our coffees, took them to the living room and sat on the couch to wait for her return. I was still thinking about her offer when she came out of the washroom still wearing the robe. It was tied tighter now but it was pretty thin and didn't leave much to the imagination. I thought, *she could wear a garbage bag and still look great.*

I said to her, "We should talk about what's going on with the power drinking."

"I guess we should," she said.

I wanted to change the atmosphere a bit, so I said, "Before we start talking, I got to ask you about the hockey boxers."

That made her smile. "I was behind in doing my laundry and the boxers were the only thing I had available to wear to work on Sunday. When I'm off work, I don't usually wear underwear at all, but at work I always do."

I felt something going on in my pants and decided to change the subject pretty fast, so I said to Stephanie, "So, tell me about the power drinking."

"Aw, Alex," she said, "I've managed homicides in the past, but this one is different. It's really gotten to me. I started managing the first murder nearly two years ago and I've hardly taken any time off work since then."

I nodded in understanding. I knew how engrossed a person could get in a case.

"The work is non-stop and the ongoing pressure I'm dealing with on a daily basis is killing me. I have regular meetings with the investigative team, the prosecutor's office and my superiors. The brass is reviewing the finances associated with the investigation keep asking me why it's been so costly. You know what it's like."

"You got to take it down a notch," I told her. "I can't imagine the pressure on you. But you're an experienced homicide investigator and you must know some other way to manage the stress. Hopefully last night was a one-off. If you make drinking like that a habit, *your* death is what the cops will be investigating," I said.

Then I advised her, "Over a lengthy investigation like this one, you have to ensure that you and your team take your regular days off—and don't cancel vacation time over it, either. You can also relieve stress by exercising and taking 'me' time. Go to a spa or go shopping. Isn't that what you girls like? Find some nice young guy and get laid. Or go and buy a new vibrator or something."

Stephanie laughed. "I have no time or interest in meeting someone just to get laid," she said, "But a new vibrator sounds good."

"Look," I said to Stephanie, serious now. "I understand what you're going through, but getting drunk in a public place is *not* the solution. The embarrassment and risk to your career isn't worth it. When I was on homicide, I sometimes drank too much at home and passed out on the couch, but at least I was at home and the only people who saw me like that were my family. But the kicker is, when you wake up, nothing really changes. All the stress is still there but now you also have a hangover to deal with."

Stephanie touched her forehead. "I definitely know about the hangover part," she said. Then she added, "I've had some drinks in the past to deal with stress, but not to this extent."

We were both silent for a moment and I decided to change the subject. "So what can you tell me about the court timeline and when I'm scheduled to testify?" I asked.

"It will probably be in two to three weeks," she said. "And remember, as a witness you are excluded from the courtroom until you've testified." Then she glanced at a clock on the wall. "I'm going to have to change and get to the office soon," she said.

I told her to go and change. "I'll drive you to your car before I go home," I said.

About ten minutes later, she came out of her bedroom dressed in a pant suit, her hair up in a bun. I told her, "You clean up pretty good." We both laughed.

I drove Stephanie to her car and as she was getting out of my truck, she stretched over and gave me a kiss on the cheek. She said, "Alex, thanks for everything. Being there for me means a lot to me, and I will never forget that you helped me out."

"No problem," I told her.

"And I have to say something else … I know it's wrong for me to try to get you to sleep with me. I don't know why I keep doing that. I feel like such an ass. Karen truly doesn't know how lucky she is to have such an honest, loyal man like you in her life."

I told Stephanie, "I'm not perfect. Karen has put up with a ton of shit from me. And you're an amazing woman. One day you will find the right person to be with."

She smiled and got out of my truck. Then she waved good bye, got into her car and left.

I drove home in painfully slow traffic, as rush hour had already started. I got home and started dinner, still thinking about Stephanie, when Karen came in from the garage. As per our usual routine, we chatted over dinner and watched television afterward. Karen must have had a busy day at work, because she never really asked me about mine.

Although I had mixed feelings about Stephanie, I felt generally good about turning her down. I treasured our friendship more than having sex with her. At times I felt like a father to her and I was glad she trusted me enough to call me from the bar, and that I was able to help her out. When I was younger, I would have jumped at the opportunity to have sex with her ... but now things are different. I treasure my marriage and family.

Over the next three weeks, nothing really exciting happened. I followed doctor's orders and took it easy; I worked my Sunday night shift and I spent the rest of the week working out and puttering around the house. I noticed some minor chest pains periodically, as well as some numbness in my hands, but I attributed that to my workouts, and thought maybe I was stretching the scar tissue on my chest. At age 63, I could still bench press over 260 pounds though I still had a bit of a gut hanging over the edge of my pants. As I like to say now, 'there are no more six packs for me, just a saggy nine pack'.

I admit I had a couple of sexual dreams about Stephanie, but every time the real good sexual stuff was about to happen, I woke up. That often happens when you dream about death, or something that could harm you. I think maybe Kobe is looking out for me. He's trying to tell me that playing with Stephanie would be like eating a stick of super-hot pepperoni. When Kobe did that, he got the runs.

CHAPTER 10

Soon, it was nearly time for the trial. It was a Friday, late afternoon, when Stephanie phoned me and told me I was scheduled to testify the following Tuesday morning, sometime after ten.

"The prosecutor wants to meet with you around eight-thirty in the morning to go through your witness statement," she said, "They're not going to call me to the stand, so I get to watch you testify." Then she said, "Oh, and Alex? Wear something pretty." I chuckled and told her I would see her early Tuesday morning.

I wasn't sure how I felt about testifying. I've been on the stand before and I've given many presentations over the course of my career, but for some reason this felt personal and it was making me a little tense thinking about it. I wanted to be a good witness. I knew I needed to be prepared. I've learned over the years that if you want to be effective in front of a group of strangers, you need to spend the time and be prepared. I started going through my files, reviewing the case and my original statement. It's nerve-wracking to go up on that stand and speak in front of a judge. I wanted to do a good job.

I spent several hours reviewing everything, making sure I could answer all the questions honestly. That's the key to being on a stand—to be honest. If you can't answer a question, tell them that you can't answer the question. If the court catches you stretching the truth, let alone flat-out lying, your credibility is lost and you can damage the outcome of a case. The jury is made up of common-sense people who can detect dishonesty.

When Karen came home I told her about my impending court date. She asked, "Will you be okay going to court ... about your heart, I mean. Do you think it will cause you stress issues and affect your heart condition?"

Since my heart surgery, Karen has really changed in how she treats me. I think she worries way too much about me having another heart attack, but she also knows me well and knows I'm pretty stubborn and have generally ignored the advice of doctors and dentists all my life. In the sack, while we used to have a pretty healthy sex life, since my heart surgery it's like she thinks I'm a china-doll or something. I understand her concern, but when we talked about it, I told her, "The only problem is in the past I did all the work. Now, if you were on top doing all the work for a change, it would be less stressful for me." She just laughed and changed the subject.

As the weekend progressed, I continued reviewing my notes and files periodically. Then I worked Sunday night as usual and made sure I got a good sleep on Monday during the day. However, on Monday night I tossed and turned thinking about going to court.

The next morning I got up, found a nice suit, made a coffee and, to beat rush hour traffic into Bisson City, I left at six in the morning to drive into town. Traffic was moving slowly, but it was okay.

I found a parking spot downtown, parked and then walked to the court house. It was still early, so on my way there I stopped by a coffee shop and grabbed another coffee. Then I made my way to the prosecutor's office.

As I entered the court, I noted that security was already in place and reporters were arriving. I looked around to see what had and who had changed. It had been about six years since I had been in court. I recognised a few faces, but there were a lot of new, younger people walking around.

I waited at the counter in the prosecutor's office until I was approached by the receptionist. I told her who I was and what case I was involved with. She escorted me into a small room that had a desk and some chairs in it. She said that the lead prosecutor, Lloyd Fox, and his assistant attorney, Samantha Matthews, would be in shortly.

I remembered Lloyd from a murder investigation I'd been involved with about ten years ago. He was a pretty good prosecutor who often got assigned to high-profile cases.

Lloyd and Samantha walked into the room a few minutes later. They hadn't changed into their court robes yet. "Good morning," said Lloyd, extending his hand. We all shook hands and as we sat down Lloyd asked me, "Have we met before?"

I said, "Yes, I'm a retired cop and you were involved with prosecuting one of my homicide cases about ten years ago."

"Yes, I remember," said Lloyd. "I thought your name looked familiar when I reviewed your witness statement. Did you have the time to review your statement?"

"Yes," I told him.

Then he said, "You do know that you're testifying as a civilian witness and can't take anything onto the stand with you, correct?" He was referring to the fact that police officers are allowed to take their notes or casebooks with them if they're called onto the stand to testify so they can refer to their notes to refresh their memories. Why civilians aren't allowed to do so is a bit of a mystery, but it would seem the courts don't want civilian witnesses reading statements word by word to the court. The only way around this for civilians is if if is their attorneys 'assist' them by introducing documents during the course of the trial.

We went over the basics and it was all pretty straight-forward. I left the office at about nine-thirty. Court started at ten and was the second witness, so I went up to courtroom number three as

Lloyd had instructed me and sat on a bench outside the room, waiting to be called. I saw Stephanie and Corey walking through the hallway full of bustling people toward me. They smiled as they approached. I shook Corey's hand and gave Stephanie a hug.

"Are you ready to testify?" she asked.

I said, "Yes."

"One of the forensic guys just finished giving evidence. You're next," she said.

"I know," I told her.

"Okay, we're going in. It's great to see you, but we want to watch your testimony. After you, Joseph Deslauriers is going to testify."

I asked, "Who is Joseph Deslauriers?"

Corey laughed. "That's your friend, Old Joe."

"That's his real name?" I asked, surprised.

"Yes, and he suits it now," said Stephanie. "We met him yesterday and got him a nice suit and a haircut, and arranged for him to stay in a hotel. He's all cleaned up for court. You won't believe the difference."

A few minutes later I saw Joe walking down the hall towards us with a young, clean-cut police officer escorting him. He had a cup of coffee in his hand and appeared to be happy, but I knew he was out of his element. I thought, *good job, Stephanie. You looked after one of your main witnesses and hopefully, with some prompting, he will do a good job testifying.*

I had to admit, I was a little concerned about Joe testifying. I wondered if he'd crack under pressure. I knew some of the experienced defence lawyers had the ability to judge a witness's personality, and if that witness was unsure of him- or herself, they attacked like sharks smelling blood.

It was announced that court was in session over the public address system and Joe sat down next to me while we waited for our names to be called. *I hope I'm called to testify before lunch,* I thought.

Joe and I chatted while the young officer who had escorted Joe down the hall hovered across the hallway, watching him. He was a key witness in the case and it was important to keep an eye on him.

Joe told me, "Alex, I'm pretty nervous about testifying. Not just because I'm going on the stand, but because no one likes a snitch on the street."

"You're not a snitch, Joe," I told him. "In fact, I think people downtown will look out for you now. No hooker wants to be killed. No pimp wants to lose money. You're doing everyone a favour by seeing that these people get lock up."

He smiled but didn't look reassured.

"Hey," I said, "I'm nervous too. Just answer the questions the best you can and if you don't know the answer, say so."

Then my name was called over the PA. "Alex McNeil, come to courtroom number three."

I stood up. "I'll see you later," I told Old Joe.

When I opened the 12-foot high doors and entered the courtroom, I started to sweat a bit. The courtroom was large and jammed-packed full of people. As I walked toward the stand, the court officer directed me to the proper side, next to the judge. I saw the two the prosecuting attorneys, Lloyd and Samantha, sitting at their table. There were two tables behind them as well, probably full of legal assistants and police officers. I noticed Stephanie and Corey sitting there. On the other side of the room were three tables full of people representing the accused, Angelo, mostly his defence team comprised of ambitious legal aid lawyers hoping this case would jump them into a lucrative career.

As I entered the stand, I nodded at the judge and said, "Good morning."

I guess he wasn't used to witnesses speaking to him. He pulled his glasses down and looked over them in surprise as he said, "Good morning, sir," back to me.

I took the Bible in my right hand and swore the oath to be

honest and to tell the truth. The judge said, "Sir you can stand or sit when you are testifying."

Because of my long legs and the small size of the witness box, I said, "I will stand."

Then the judge said, "Counsel, I need a moment," as he went through some documents. I didn't like the delay. I started getting a little nervous standing in front of all those people. I looked around and saw Stephanie smiling at me. She discreetly gave me a little wink. I was able to crack a slight smile back.

Once, years ago, I'd been in court because Stephanie had been subpoenaed. She was nervous, so before court I told her that, while she would be testifying before a fair and reasonable judge, the only problem is that *this* judge always wore blue eyeliner, and usually too much of it. I told her, "Just make sure you don't stare at her if she has too much makeup on." Sure enough, that judge was wearing too much blue makeup. Stephanie tried not to look, and looked at me instead. I thought a little added pressure on Stephanie would be good for her and so, while she was testifying, I started rubbing my eyes when she looked in my direction. After court she told me that she just about broke out in laughter, and that one day she was going to get me back. I wondered, *will today be the day?*

Finally, the judge was ready. He nodded to Lloyd to begin questioning me. Lloyd walked me through my story in a linear way. He started with my police background and homicide experience. At this point, I just agreed with his statements, saying, 'yes, sir' or 'that's correct'. When it came time to tell what I saw that night in the laneway, I described the vehicle in the laneway, the shiny thing in the back of the van and the yellow sticker in the rear window. I told the court about finding the victim and that she had a bag over her head but was still alive, though barely. He asked if I could identify the people I'd seen near the van and I answered 'no'. He asked for any details and I said, "All I can say with certainty was that from a distance they appeared to be very similar in size, between five-foot-six and five-eight. Both were stocky. One had a longer plaid coat on and the other had a jacket that might have been a jean jacket."

Then Lloyd asked the judge for a few minutes to review his notes. As I waited to be released from the stand, I looked around the courtroom and caught Stephanie's eye again. She had a slight smile on her face and winked again. Then she discreetly reached under her suit jacket with one hand and fondled her breast. No one else was looking at her but me, and I felt myself flush. I thought, *what a bitch, she finally got me back after all these years.*

Then Lloyd said he had no more questions, which drew my attention back to the trial. The defense attorney had just one clarifying question, asking me, "Can you identify my client as being one of the persons seen at the van?"

I said, "No, sir. I cannot positively identify anyone who was near the van."

"I have no more questions," he said.

There was no cross-examination by Lloyd and I was told to step down. Lloyd then asked the Judge if it was a good time to have a morning break. The Judge said it was and he and jury departed the courtroom.

I went out to the hallway. Joe was still sitting on the wooden bench, waiting for his turn to testify. He looked anxious. I sat down beside him and said, "Don't worry, it will be over soon."

"Thanks," he said.

Stephanie came over, sat down beside me and whispered in my ear, "It took a long time, but I got you!"

I said, "You're naughty and you deserved to be spanked."

She said with a smirk, "The hockey team boxers were also in the courtroom watching you testify."

I laughed, thinking about her boxers. "Is it laundry day again?" I asked. Then I asked her if we had enough time to grab a coffee and she said, 'yes'. I asked Joe and Corey, "Do you want us to bring you back a coffee?" They both said 'yes'.

As we walked downstairs to the coffee shop, I said, "I'm interested in seeing Joe testify. I hope he does well. He's key to winning this thing."

"We worked with him a lot," she told me. "I think he's ready."

Then I said, "I don't plan to come every day, but I really want to see Sophie testify. And if Angelo's lawyer puts him on the stand, I also want to watch him."

"No problem, Alex," said Stephanie. "I'll make sure to keep you in the loop for the dates."

We grabbed the coffees and went back upstairs to the hallway outside the courtroom. We chatted for a bit and I told Old Joe, "Don't worry about testifying. I'll be in the courtroom watching and encouraging you, okay?"

Joe smiled and said, "Okay, Alex, thanks for the support."

We went back into the courtroom and I was able to grab a seat beside Stephanie and Corey. As the courtroom filled up, up front I noticed three rows of seats reserved for the victims' families. Some of the women sitting there were holding tissue and were clearly the mothers of the victims. I noticed a nicely dressed black couple who appeared to be in their mid- to late-forties, probably Sally Armstrong's parents. I heard another couple speaking French and assumed they were related to Mary St. Cyr.

The judge and jury returned. The judge asked the prosecuting attorney who the next witness was. Lloyd had the court officer page Old Joe. As Joe entered the courtroom, I felt nervous for him. He had cleaned up pretty good, but he still had that street demeanor. I hoped the defense attorney wouldn't pick up on it or he'd beat the crap out of him.

Presenting evidence in court is like a high-level chess game. The police disclose evidence to the prosecutor who reviews it and develops a court strategy. The prosecutor then must share the evidence with the defense, although they generally vet out any personal information about witnesses. When the defense gets the evidence, he or she looks for weaknesses in the investigation so they can build reasonable doubt in the minds of the jury. They just have to sway the jury enough so they're not sure about a conviction; unlike the prosecutor, they don't have to prove anything.

All this had been done leading up to the trial. Now it was time to see how it would unfold. Lloyd slowly drew information out of Joe with some well-crafted questions and Joe did a pretty good job describing what he'd seen. He stated firmly that he had watched the Martinos remove a body from their van, carry it to the river's edge and dump it into the water. He said he clearly recognized the Martinos, and their vehicle, because he knew them and had purchased hot dogs from them. He also said he'd seen them angrily arguing more than once and that they didn't appear to like each other much. When Lloyd asked Joe if he recognized one of the Martinos in the courtroom, he looked at and clearly pointed out Angelo, who was seated next to his attorney.

I knew Lloyd had avoided asking Joe about the specifics of any argument because if he said too much about how violent Sophie was, it might sway the jury into seeing her as the aggressor and discredit her witness creditability. She was the star witness against Angelo, so he didn't want that.

Angelo's defense attorney was named was Edward Williams. I looked over at him; he was clean cut and when he spoke he was very articulate. His legal assistants sat behind him, highly organized, with files and papers neatly stacked on the desk. One of the assistants had a laptop open and was busy typing. I thought, *wow, courtroom technology has certainly changed over the years.* The judge, prosecutor and defense attorney were also all busy typing into their laptops, and I knew the police disclosure was now given electronically too.

Soon it was Ed's turn to question Joe. I was sure Ed's legal argument would be that although his client, Angelo, was involved in the murders, he was actually a victim who was forced into doing it by his controlling and murderous wife. I was right. Like a skilled surgeon, he went through the evidence bit by bit, slowly clarifying questions until he got Joe to say on a number of occasions that in every interaction he had observed between Sophie and Angelo, Sophie appeared to be the aggressor.

Joe ended up testifying that Sophie was a loud, mean, abusive aggressive person and that he had observed her ordering and pushing Angelo around and, to his credit, when Lloyd cross-examined him on this, he stuck to his story, stating that Sophie was the aggressor. Joe wasn't a great witness, but I think he was a good witness. When he finished his testimony, court was adjourned for a one o'clock lunch break.

I met Joe, Stephanie and Corey in the hallway. I shook Joe's hand. "You did a good job testifying," I told him.

"Thanks," Joe said, and then he departed with a police escort. I think he was just happy just to get out of the courthouse.

Stephanie and Corey said that they had to go back to the office. I asked Stephanie if I could speak to her for a minute.

"Sure," she said. Corey told her he would meet her back at the office. "What's up?" asked Stephanie.

"I'm really struggling with some elements of this case," I told her. "I know you're super busy and have to be here every day, but I'm wondering if you have some time to meet with me to talk about a couple of things."

She thought for minute or two and then said, "Okay, I'll make a deal with you.

"A deal?" I asked.

"Yes," she said. "There's no court on Friday and I planned to take the day off, but we could get together instead. Not at my office, though. That isn't the right place. If anyone realized I was discussing elements of the investigation with a civilian, I'd be in shit. How about you come by my condo around ten?"

I told her, "I'm not sure it's a good idea for me to go to your place."

She promised with a smile that she would keep her hands off me. I asked her, "So what is the deal?"

She looked directly into my eyes and said, "If you come to my place, I will answer every question you have for me about the serial killings … but the deal is that you have to also answer one question of mine."

"Well that's intriguing," I said. "Is it an above-the-belt question?"

She just laughed. "I guess you'll have to find out," she said.

"Okay then," I said. "I'll take that deal." Then I asked her, "Who's testifying on Wednesday and Thursday?"

"It's all going to be forensic identification officers testifying about the seizure and handling of the evidence, chain of custody stuff. You know."

"Good. Make sure you tell me when Angelo and Sophie testify. I don't want to miss that."

"You know I will," she said.

I told her I would see her on Friday and we hugged and said good bye. I wondered if I had made the right decision about going to her place. She had made some pretty clear sexual advances in the last little while and I have to admit, every time we saw each other, I thought about it too. *Don't play with fire,* Alex, I thought, but my entire drive home, all I could think about was Stephanie. Part of me thought I should go for it. *She knows I'm married and she's not really looking for a commitment. She probably just wants to have sex …*

I started to imagine it and had to suddenly slam on my brakes when I nearly hit a stopped car in front of me. That jolted me out of my fantasy and suddenly I thought about how wrong it would be to sleep with Stephanie. We were long-time friends and I respected her as a police officer and a friend. I knew she was exhausted from working on this murder investigation and I also knew she was under a lot of pressure and needed a friend. *Maybe I'm the only person she's got who can offer her the support she needs.* I wasn't sure if Stephanie could get that kind of support from family or friends.

Then I also thought about Karen and how hurt she would be if she found out I had slept with Stephanie. I know how hurt *I* would be if I found out Karen was having an affair behind my back. I was also really concerned that if I had sex with Stephanie, it would change our friendship. We have joked around and harmlessly flirted with each other for years, but we've never touched each other with sexual desire, at least not when we worked together. Obviously, I've looked at her body checked her out, but that's it.

The rest of the drive home was uneventful and by the time I walked in the door, I'd refocused my mind on the murder trial. I really believed what Joe said about Sophie being the aggressor.

I got home and had just started making dinner. When Karen walked in the door, all of a sudden I felt so guilty. We had been together so long—more than 30 years—so why was I thinking so much about Stephanie? I looked at her and I saw how beautiful she was. Karen had stood by me and supported me during my entire policing career, and we had lived together relatively happily in the same house all our lives. She was a great mother and a great wife. Why was I letting this whole thing with Stephanie get to me?

Karen asked, "How was court? I heard about you testifying on the news." They don't allow cameras in the courtroom, but news reporters take notes on every word spoken in court.

I said, "I think that it went okay. I told what I knew and that was all I could do." We had dinner and watched television for a while before going to bed. I tried to snuggle up to Karen and she said that she was tired and wanted to go to sleep.

The next morning I had coffee with Karen and kissed her good bye when she left for work. Then I went to the gym for a couple of hours. After that, I did a few things around the house and worked on the Plymouth until I got tired. I was still thinking about the murders, so after taking a break, I got on the computer and went through my files again. I had quite a bit of information and it took me nearly two hours to read through it. Then I sat back and rubbed my eyes.

"Kobe, old boy," I said to the walls, "This ball is not bouncing straight. I know that woman is lying."

Although I didn't know all the details or what hold back evidence the police had, I still struggled with Sophie being a witness for the prosecution. She was a murderous bitch and she was getting off light by making a deal. To me, the evidence more than showed they'd committed every murder together, and I believed they should have been charged jointly for all seven murders.

I banged my fist down on the dining room table, frustrated at the thought of such an evil person not being accountable and suddenly, pain shot up my arm to my chest. I started sweating and could hardly breathe. I knew I was having another heart attack, and this one seemed really strong. I was just about to call 911 when the pain subsided a bit. I skipped taking aspirin and went right for a double dose of my medication.

After a minute or so I felt well enough to make my way to the living room and lay down on the couch, were I stayed for the next few hours. I knew I was lucky not to have dropped dead and that I should call an ambulance, but I didn't. Instead, I decided to make a follow-up appointment with Dr. Burns for early next week.

When I finally got off the couch, I called Dr. Burns' office and spoke to the receptionist. She said it was good timing, as I was due for my monthly appointment anyway. Then when Karen got home, I told her about the doctor's appointment and also that I was going down to Bisson to meet with Stephanie to discuss the investigation and court. "Alex, you have to take it easy," she said.

"I'm not going to court every day," I told her, "I just want to be there when Angelo and Sophie testify. I don't like the way the prosecutor set up their case."

Karen looked at me and said, "Alex, has this court case got anything to do with you booking a doctor's appointment?"

I lied and said, "I don't think so, but I'm not feeling one hundred percent." She looked worried.

On Friday morning I got up, got dressed, had coffee with Karen and then headed downtown to Stephanie's place. I wondered, *what does she want to ask me? And can my heart take it?*

CHAPTER II

The drive to downtown Bisson City was pretty good. I grabbed a couple of coffees before I got to Stephanie's place, then I rang her door buzzer and she buzzed me in. As I walked down the hall towards her condo, she opened her door and surprised me. I couldn't believe how different and good she looked when she was off duty. Instead of a business suit and a bun, she wore tight jeans, a sweater and her hair was loose, long and wavy. I couldn't help but notice that the sweater was form-fitting and short, ending just above her navel and showing a little skin.

"Hey, you," she said with a smile.

"Hi Stephanie," I said, handing her a coffee.

She hugged me and said, "Thanks for bringing the coffee, but I made some!"

"Refills, I guess," I said.

We sat in the living room to talk. She brought the extra coffee and some finger-type sandwiches and set them down on the coffee table. Then she sat down across from me in a wing chair.

"So, how are you doing, Alex," She asked. "You look like you lost more weight."

"In total I've lost over 30 pounds," I told her, adding, "I have the odd bad day, but overall I'm pretty good."

Stephanie jokingly said, "You're getting leaner and hotter."

I told her, "You should get some glasses." We both laughed.

Then Stephanie said, "Let's get to it, Alex. Ask me your questions about the investigation."

"Well, like I said, I'm struggling with the prosecutor's decision to only charge Angelo and to let Sophie plead accessory after the fact. What was the actual deal with Sophie?"

Stephanie sighed. "It's like this," she said, "After we reviewed all the evidence, the case was a little weaker than we thought. Charging them jointly with all seven counts of first-degree murder was an all-or-nothing shot that the prosecutor didn't want to chance."

"How weak *was* the case?" I asked.

"There was very little direct evidence against either of them, with the exception of Joe's eye witness account and your evidence. There was no DNA from the Martinos at any of the crime scenes, or on any of the victims. The plastic bags did have both of their finger prints on them, but there was no direct evidence that they had suffocated the victims, except for their own self-serving statements. Ed figured the defense might argue that the plastic bags could have been handled by them and then discarded, so that was kind of shaky. And there was no direct evidence either of them had actually killed the victims."

"That sucks," I said.

"Also, when the steel pipe was forensically tested, it only had the victims' DNA on it. There was no handler DNA profiles found, so no evidence to suggest Sophie or Angelo handled the pipe. And neither of them copped to anything. They both provided similar statements. Both admitted they were present and involved with all the murders; both admitted they had disposed of the bodies together; and both said they were forced to participate in the murders. The issue is that *both* of them are crying 'victim'. The only truth, I think, is that they traumatized each other for over 20 years, getting drunk and beating the crap out of one another. But ultimately, it boiled down to 'he said, she said' and so this is why it was handled the way it was."

"I see," I said.

"Don't think there weren't mixed feelings in the prosecutor's office. No one is certain if a jury will be able to determine which Martino is telling the truth. There is very little direct evidence and it could cause a hung jury or reasonable doubt. It's dicey."

Stephanie said her team spent months and months investigating the Martinos, trying to determine who the main aggressor was. They searched their home again but could find no decisive evidence.

"And did you know they both failed the polygraph tests we gave them?"

"You gave them polygraph tests?"

"Yes." She looked at me slyly. "I know polygraph tests can't be used in court in Canada, so stop looking so confused. We did the tests anyway, to lead them into an interrogation type of interview. It didn't work. However, we did find out that Angelo has an undiagnosed mental health issue. He consented to psychological testing and that confirmed that he was prone to violent outbursts unless he took prescribed medication."

"Well that's a nail in the coffin for Angelo," I said. "But what about Sophie? I still think she's getting off lightly."

"As you know, Sophie presented herself as a victim. It was a difficult decision to let her run with that, but the prosecutor wanted to ensure *someone* was held accountable for the deaths of seven people, if for no other reason than to bring closure to the victims' families and friends. And even if she walks in three years, she's off the streets for three years ... and hopefully Angelo gets a lot more time than that."

"So what deal was made with Sophie to get her to plead guilty and become a witness?" I asked.

"As I told you, she'll get seven years and she'll be eligible for parole after serving three."

"Holy shit," I said. "With time served, she could be out in a year!"

"I know," said Stephanie glumly.

We had been talking for over an hour and the coffee and sandwiches were long gone. Stephanie said, "It's time for a pee break. There's some whiskey in the kitchen cabinet. Why don't you make us a couple of drinks?"

I made two large rye whiskeys on the rocks and sat them on the coffee table. Stephanie returned and sat down on the couch next to me. We banged our classes together and said 'cheers'.

"So, do you have more questions?" she asked me.

"No, not really," I said. "But I'm still not happy with Sophie's plea deal. I want to attend court and to listen both of their testimonies.

"I know! You're a broken record," she said. "I'll tell you when they are scheduled to testify." Then it was Stephanie's turn. "Can I now ask my question?" she asked.

I said, "Sure."

She said, "Please do not interrupt me until I finish talking. And before we start, could you grab the bottle of whiskey from the kitchen and bring it to the living room? This might be a long discussion."

I grabbed the bottle from the kitchen and returned to the living room, wondering what she was about to tell me, or ask me.

Looking down at the floor, she started by saying, "Alex, I don't know what is wrong with me. I've dedicated all my time to my career. I've climbed the ranks of the homicide unit and been promoted to the rank of inspector. I've been very successful investigating and managing homicide investigations. However, my personal life is a mess. I've sacrificed my personal life for my job."

I remained silent, waiting for her to go on.

She said, "With my career and the long and unusual hours I work, I can never find the right guy to be with. Guys never seem to understand that I can't always be available to go out. They don't understand why they can't spend more time with me. Sometimes I'm with someone and my phone rings and I just have to drop everything and suddenly go to work. And after that, boom ... relationship over."

"The job does take over your life," I agreed.

"I'm talking to you because you understand," she said. "I have a brother and sister. My sister doesn't understand the pressure, my brother doesn't really care, and there is nobody really close to me at work that I can talk to. Besides, I can't spill my guts about personal feelings to co-workers. They'd think I was weak. It's so bad that I have not slept with a guy for nearly four years. Vibrators are okay, but they're no substitute for being touched by someone who loves you. I need more."

"I understand," I said. I couldn't imagine not having someone to hold me for four long years.

"It's not the fact I'm not having sex, it's that I don't have anyone to be close to. You're pretty much my closest friend."

"That's pretty desperate," I said.

She didn't smile. Instead, she said, "I want to enjoy my life with someone I can have a relationship with who also understands my commitment to being a cop. I want to be with a guy I can talk to and confide in, someone understands me and maybe who can even support me through the difficult times at work."

"I get it," I said.

"Did you know that the only physical contact I've had with a male in the last year was when you and I hugged? I can't even explain how that felt to me. But, that having been said, I'm really embarrassed about the way I've been trying to get you to have sex with me. Especially the way I pranced around in front of you in my see-through robe. But I just wanted so much to be intimate, and close to you."

She looked away from me and to lighten up the conversation, I told her she could wear with ever she wanted around me. "I'm getting old, but I'm not blind. You're a beautiful woman with a great personality and you have a lot to offer *any* guy. Guys should be lining up at your front door to go out with you," I told her.

Then I touched her shoulder gently. "Stephanie," I said, "If I was a little younger and wasn't married, I would be all over you. And I hope you don't take my flirtatious comments the wrong way."

"No, I enjoy the flirting. You're the only person who flirts with me."

"As soon as this trial is over, you need to take some time off," I told her. "But other than that, have a little faith in yourself. Don't change for anyone, because you're an amazing woman. I'm sure if you relax a little, you'll meet that special guy. You just need to make a space for him, I guess. But you and I ... well, we're always going to be special friends, no matter what."

She nodded, but she looked sad and I didn't know if it was the whiskey, but her heartache made me want to cry. To the world she was Inspector Stephanie Foster, a well-respected homicide investigator who ran a unit of 40 police officers; who successfully managed investigations; who made arrests; who was professional and yet sensitive to co-workers and victims. *Wonder woman.* To me, she was Stephanie Foster, my friend of 15 years. Under that tough police exterior was a woman who just wanted to feel secure and be loved.

"I feel the same about you, Alex," she said. Then she asked, "And here's my question." My ears perked up, curious. She hesitated a moment before she said, "I wonder if you'd consider doing something for me that might sound a little unusual."

"Sure, what is it?" I asked.

"Come with me to my bedroom," she said. She grabbed my hand and I resisted. She said, "I don't want you to have sex with me. I just want you to hold me and cuddle me for a while. We'll keep our clothes on and just lay next to each other." I didn't know what to say. This was dangerous territory. She looked me in the eye and I could see the misery there. Then she said, "I just need to feel another human's warmth ... to feel the security of a man's arms wrapped around me for a while. Can you do that for me, Alex?"

I was a little leery, but I also felt great compassion for her. The serial killings had burnt her out. She was exhausted and it was obvious she felt very insecure.

"Sure," I said, against my better judgement.

We went into her bedroom and laid on top of the bed covers next to each other. I curled up behind her and put my arm around her in the classic spoon position. She pulled my hand into her stomach and squeezed it and said, "Thank you."

And that was it. Although our bodies were touching, it was in a sensual rather than sexual way. There was no passion, but there was great need—a basic, instinctive, human need to feel safe and secure. As I lay next to her, I noticed she smelt nice and at times when my hand grazed the skin of her stomach, it was so soft. It felt good lying next to her. I didn't allow my mind to wander further than kindness, but it was a struggle.

We lay on the bed holding each other for an hour or so, talking a bit about our families and friends. No matter what position we shifted into, we continued holding each other. If I lay on my back she would put her head on my chest and wrap her arm around my waist. Some of the time we didn't even talk. I'm sure we both dozed off a couple of times.

There was a lot of body contact and though I tried to keep a little space between us, her breasts and butt brushed against me on number of occasions. Soon my body started to betray me and despite my best intentions, I started getting aroused. It was the first time I *really* had an urge to have sex with her … but it was so special that I also didn't want to ruin it.

After a while, Stephanie fell into a deep sleep. She snored a bit, which I thought was cute. I wondered, *how long has it been since she has been able to have a good night's sleep?* I was feeling pretty drowsy myself, but I looked at the clock on the wall and saw that it was approaching four in the afternoon. I could have just lain there with her all night, but I had a whole other life to get back to. I leaned over and kissed Stephanie on the forehead.

"This had been really nice, but I have to get up and get going,"

I said softly. She seemed a little startled but said she understood. "I'm sorry I have to go. And I'm also sorry that certain parts of me may have bucked my willpower and poked you a little."

She giggled and said, "A few of my parts might have accidently brushed against you on purpose."

She walked me to the front door and reassured me once more that she would call me when she found out the date of Sophie and Angelo's testimonies. Then she said, "Thank you," again.

I hugged her. "Good bye," I said. I added, "You are really special to me, Stephanie … but I can't come back to your condo anymore. However nice it was, it was inappropriate, at least to me. Are you okay with that?" She looked disappointed, but she nodded. Although I didn't say it, I thought to myself … *next time I won't be able to control myself, and I can't do that to Karen.*

Stephanie stood on her tip toes and kissed me on the cheek. She said, "You're a great friend and quite a guy."

I left her condo and went down to my truck. As I drove home, I felt the 'walk of shame' syndrome. We didn't have sex, but I felt guilty as hell. I don't think many people, especially spouses, understand a close, strong friendship between a male and a female. For that matter, I'm not sure I did. I know I would be pretty pissed off if Karen cuddled with some guy. *Perhaps I crossed the line.* No, I *did* cross the line.

Nevertheless, I hoped that spending that time with Stephanie helped her come down to earth. I thought maybe she should consider transferring to a less demanding job. Perhaps *then* she would have the opportunity to meet a nice guy and enjoy her life.

I got home just as Karen did. "Hi," she said. "What did you get up to today?"

I said I'd met Stephanie and that we'd spent most of the day talking about the serial killings. Good thing she never asked me where we did our talking. "I have a better understanding of why the prosecutor made the deal with Sophie," I told her, "But I still don't agree with it. I think Sophie will reoffend when she gets out of jail. You don't go from being a serial killer to singing in the choir overnight."

"You better not get worked up over it," Karen said. "There is a highly trained team of people using their knowledge of the law working on this. They don't need your opinions too. And you don't need to give them."

I smiled at her gentle admonishment, but ignored it, instead saying, "Sometimes deals are made too quickly to bring closure to the victim's families and to stop the incessant media attention."

"And you think that's what happened here?" she asked.

"I think it might have," I said.

I had to take my Sunday night trash man shift off, as my appointment with Dr. Burns was on Monday morning. I didn't eat much Sunday night in preparation for my appointment and I decided I was going to tell him about the mini-heart attack I'd had. Although I'd been feeling pretty good the last few days, I was worried about that attack. I wondered if it had something to do with my blocked artery. *Is it normal to have these mini chest pains, I wondered?*

I got up early Monday morning, had coffee with Karen and drove down to Bisson City. Although I was going to be way too early, I didn't want to sit in bumper to bumper traffic. I got to the hospital around ten, and the receptionist recognized me and greeted me with a smile. "How is everything?" she asked. "How are you feeling?"

I said, "Overall, pretty good. But I need to ask Dr. Burns if it's possible or normal to have mini heart attacks."

She asked, "What happened?"

I told her about my attack the previous week and she looked at me and said, "Alex, you *cannot* take a chance like that! You could have died!" Then she immediately scheduled a blood test and an electrocardiogram for me. "You're getting these tests right now, and I've moved your consultation with Dr. Burns to one o'clock," she said.

I was a little shocked by how concerned she was. *I better start taking this more seriously,* I thought. And then I was whisked away for some tests, which took two hours.

After that, I was taken back to the waiting room and when my name was called I went into Dr. Burns' office. He said, "Alex! Hello. Good to see you. My receptionist mentioned the discussion you had with her and that she sent you for some extra tests. I've been reviewing the test results and it appears you *did* have a mild heart attack, more than one, it would seem. Your heart is still repairing itself from the surgery and the blocked artery is causing stress. However, if it's possible, I still want to wait at least three months before scheduling a second surgery. We need that time to make sure your heart and new arteries are strong."

Then he gave me a few pamphlets about proper eating, exercising and stress avoidance. Each pamphlet included the signs to look for when you are having a heart attack. I thought, *with what I know now, I could probably write my own pamphlet.*

"It appears that one artery is blocked about 85 to 90 percent," Dr. Burns told me. "Usually if one of my patients has a 70 percent blockage, I try to get them into surgery right away." Then he explained that while you cannot unclog blocked arteries through diet and exercise, you *can* avoid further plaque buildup.

"Alex, you've already had a triple by-pass and you still have an issue with a blocked artery," he concluded. "Please take it easy and follow my instructions. Take your medication, and if you have any issues call an ambulance." He issued me another prescription with instructions and told me he wanted to see me every two to three weeks.

On the way home, I decided to grab some coffees and stop at Karen's work to tell her right away and in person what Dr. Burns had said. She is the manager of a pool of about 20 legal assistants in a large corporation, so I grabbed six coffees before I stopped by. When I got there, I waited in the front lobby as the security officer phoned her. When she came out to see me, she said, "This is quite a surprise. You hardly ever stop by."

I said, "I wanted to tell you what Dr. Burns said."

We sat down on a bench seat in the lobby and I told her everything. She was speechless and her eyes started to tear up. I realized I should have waited and told her at home. She said, "Alex, I love you and I don't want to lose you, so smarten the fuck up," in a voice I had not heard in a long time, a voice she used to use with the kids when they were younger. And then she actually punched me in the arm and said, "If you start feeling any pains, or anything like a heart attack about to start, call an ambulance! Promise me," she said.

Like a kid, I looked down and said, "Yes, dear." Then I gave her the coffees, kissed her on the check, said good bye and went home. I knew she was right.

At home, I made dinner for us and we watched television until about ten. When we got into bed, Karen wanted to cuddle for a while. We cuddled and ended up making love. It had been a while, but it was certainly very nice.

In the morning, we had coffee as usual and when Karen was about to leave for work, she came over and gave me a kiss. Over the years, we haven't usually kissed each other good bye, but lately that's changed. She said, "Please look after yourself. I'm really worried about you."

"Okay," I said.

I went to work on Monday night because I had taken Sunday off. The night was pretty normal. I grabbed a coffee at Pete's and said hello to the girls on the corner. I heard some of them say, "Hi, trash man."

I finished the shift and went home to find I'd missed Karen; she'd already gone to work. I passed out and had a good sleep until the phone rang. It was Stephanie. She asked, "Are you okay? You sound groggy."

"I worked Monday night instead of Sunday night," I said. "I was just waking up."

She asked, "Can you talk for a few minutes?"

"Sure," I said.

Stephanie said Sophie was scheduled to testify against Angelo on Thursday and that they expected her testimony, including cross examination, to last a day. "Thanks for letting me know," I said. "I'm going to that."

Stephanie said she had to tell me something else. "I can't keep a secret anymore," she said.

"What are you talking about?" I asked.

"Well, Karen called me early this morning and told me about your new heart problems. She's really worried about you and wasn't sure if it was a good idea for you to attend court and watch the proceedings because you get so wrapped up in it. So you should think about that."

I told Stephanie that I was being more careful and not to worry. "Don't tell Karen I told you," she said. "I don't want her to think I'm a snitch." I said I wouldn't mention the phone call and the Stephanie said, "Come to the police station around eight-thirty and we can walk up to court together."

I said, "That would be great." The police station was about ten minutes away from the courthouse.

Then her tone of her voice changed. It got softer. She said, "Alex, thanks for being there for me last week. You had my back when I was dealing with some issues. I'll never forget it."

I said, "That's what old partners do for each other."

I took it easy for the next little while, eating healthy vegetables during the day and going for a couple of walks. With the recent attack, I decided I better not go back to the gym for a while, so I didn't. I told Karen that I was going down to Bisson to see Sophie testify and she wasn't too happy with me. There was definitely no cuddling that night.

The next morning of Sophie's testimony, I got up and had

coffee with Karen as usual. She made a point of telling me to stay calm when I heard the testimony. I told her I would try to. Then I left and drove down to Bisson City. On the way there, I wondered if Stephanie and team had contacted mental health specialists to evaluate each Martino's mental state and whether psychological and psychiatric reviews had been conducted. I further wondered if these specialists somehow determine which Martino was more prone to violence, or who was telling the truth.

I met Corey and Stephanie in the lobby of the police station. I hadn't seen Corey for a while, but he seemed happy to see me. As we walked up the steps of the courthouse, I thought how professional they both looked. The homicide unit officers had the reputation of being the best dressed unit in the police service. The males were always clean cut and wore the nicest, most expensive suits and the females, like Stephanie, were immaculately groomed and exhibited professionalism in everything they did. Stephanie set the standard for how the female officers in the homicide unit should dress, maintaining femininity with just the right amount of make-up, but projecting strength with a ladies' suit and sensible shoes she could run in if she had to. Today, she looked fabulous, but as I said, she could look good in a trash bag. When we used to work together, no one *ever* looked at me.

But beyond her looks and style, Stephanie was simply a fantastic cop. When we worked together, she had been able to get a record number of confessions and her interviewing and interrogation technique made her an excellent interviewer. Stephanie ensured that she did as much preliminary work as she could prior to any interview and then, with her soft-spoken voice, beauty and charm, she was usually able to build rapport with anyone and get a confession. I don't think any of the suspects, particularly the males, even had a chance.

Stephanie and Corey were both wearing their firearms. I had always had a thing for plainclothes female cops with guns. The guns just hung loosely off their hips in provocative way that turns me on.

When entered the courthouse, I noticed the hallways were jam-packed. Stephanie and Corey had to go and meet with the assistant prosecutor before court. "We'll reserve a seat in the courtroom for you," Stephanie told me. "Just wait in the hallway until court starts."

As I waited, a black man approached me and said, "Excuse me, are you the person they call 'the trash man'?"

"Yes, but my real name is Alex," I responded.

"Sorry to mix up your name," he said, "I'd like to talk to you, if that's okay." I nodded. He introduced himself as Edward Armstrong, Sally Armstrong's father. "And this is my wife, Roberta." I shook both their hands.

I said, "I'm sorry I had never had the opportunity to offer my condolences to you."

Edward said, "Thank you. We're still struggling with the loss of Sally. But that's not what I want to talk about. I just wanted to thank you."

I asked him, "What for?"

He said, "When Sally ran away and started working the streets, once every three or four months she would call us just to say 'hi' and to tell us she was okay. One time she called and talked about someone called 'the trash man'. She said this 'trash man' had gone out of his way to help her out and we were confused as to who, or what, he was. She told us you asked for nothing in return. It really impacted her."

I told them, "She was a sweet kid and I just wanted her to get a leg up. I knew that somewhere she had parents who loved her. I hoped she'd get her act together one day and go back home." They smiled at me sadly and I said, "You had a beautiful daughter who went a little astray. All teenagers do that. I didn't know her that well, but the times I spoke with her made me believe she was a good person. I know Sally loved both of you very much."

Edward shook my hand and said, "I'm not really sure how you helped her, but thank you." Roberta gave me a hug. Then they held each other's hands as they walked away down the hallway.

It was announced that court was about to start, so I went inside the courtroom. Corey and Stephanie had saved me a seat, as promised. I sat down and immediately looked at Sophie, who was sitting next to the prosecutor. Someone in had taken the time to clean her up. Although she was still in custody, she was wearing civilian clothing, her hair styled and she was wearing makeup. I looked closely at her and thought it funny that she was wearing a high-neck top. I knew from seeing pictures on the Internet that the top was just high enough to cover up the tattoo she had on her neck.

A few minutes later, Angelo was escorted into the courtroom and his handcuffs were removed. He was seated next to his lawyer. Although he was wearing a suit, he still looked a little scruffy. I didn't see either of them look at each other.

The court officer called Sophie's name and she walked up to the box to be sworn in. She placed her hand on the Bible and swore to tell the truth. I thought, *she's a devil in disguise.* I still couldn't believe they'd made such a deal with her. I believed she had the ability to bullshit a twelve-member jury, thought I thought it might be harder for her to bullshit a judge.

The prosecuting attorney started going through the evidence with her. It was obvious he, or a member of his team, had prepared her to testify against Angelo. Sophie answered basic questions about her background and her relationship with Angelo. Then Lloyd introduced into evidence the original, digitally recorded statement she'd made to police after her arrest.

After the court listened to her recorded statement, Lloyd asked her some clarifying questions. She basically repeated what she'd said in her original interview with the police. Her parents were suffering in the old country and so the family immigrated to Canada. Her parents and Angelo's parents were friends who'd had gone through the war together and had survived the German occupation. Once in Canada, their parents had purchased homes near each other. As young adults, Angelo and she had started dating. They got married and for a wedding gift, both sets of parents had chipped in to purchase them a home. In her recorded statement, she'd spoken about how Angelo started abusing her shortly after they got married. She fleshed that out a little and said that, while they both regularly consumed alcohol, he was a violent alcoholic who constantly yelled at her and beat her up. Sophie also said he'd chained her up in the basement numerous times. She said she had been abused for over 20 years until finally she'd just accepted the fact that it was normal to be abused and beaten.

I listened to her testimony closely. I didn't believe her. I had trouble accepting that she was an abused woman. From my police experience, I knew that abused women spoke differently and used different words. Abused women, when they testify, show shame about their past and look down or away. On the stand, they relive their bad experiences and usually break down crying. Further, she repeated her statement almost word for word, to the point that I thought everyone in the courtroom must realize how much it had been rehearsed.

Sophie stated that about six months before the first murder, Angelo had chained her up in the basement. Then he'd called for an escort and a twenty-year-old prostitute had arrived at the house. There was a conversation at the front door, and from the basement she had heard what sounded like footsteps going up to the second-floor bedroom. After about 20 minutes, she said she heard Angelo yelling at the girl. The girl yelled back, saying 'it's not my fault you can't get a hard-on. I have done my best and I want to get paid'. The argument continued, Sophie said, until she heard a noise that sounded like someone falling down the stairs. Then she heard Angelo slapping and hitting the girl and telling her to get out of the house. The next morning, Angelo undid her handcuffs and she went upstairs to find a poorly-cleaned mess of blood near the front door of the house and at the base of the stairs leading to the second floor.

Then she repeated the rest of her original story about how Angelo had killed the victims and she had been forced to help him. Sophie described how mad Angelo got when he found out Bobbi Thompson had male genitals. Sophie said that Angelo had grabbed a knife from the hot dog cart and impulsively stabbed and cut him. She also explained that they had grabbed Sally Armstrong by mistake. They didn't know she was black, as she had long blonde hair that night.

Angelo, Sophie said, would pick the victims and they all had to look like the prostitute who had been at their house. She said Angelo was a violent, bitter man who remained upset that a woman had made him feel like he wasn't a man.

Court proceeded through the morning break then broke for lunch. I met Stephanie and Corey in the hallway and I told both of them I *still* didn't believe Sophie was telling the truth. I asked Stephanie, "Did you locate the original prostitute who was in that house with Angelo?"

She said, "No. We were able to track down the escort service, Delightful Treats, that employed her. Unfortunately, they didn't keep proper records on the girls. They said her street name was Sunshine and that Sunshine had mysteriously disappeared and never picked up her last pay from them."

"Shit," I said.

"Forensics ripped apart the flooring inside the front door and found blood droplets under the hardwood flooring. They were able to develop a DNA profile from the blood, but it wasn't in the national DNA data bank system, so it was a dead end for us."

Corey and Stephanie went back to their office for lunch. I grabbed a coffee and went for a short walk in the downtown area. When court resumed, Sophie finished her testimony. Now it was Angelo's lawyer, Ed Williams', turn to cross examine Sophie.

Ed immediately questioned Sophie about the deal she'd made

with the prosecutor's office. "You entered a guilty plea for being an accessory to murder after the fact for all *seven* murders. I think you got the deal of a lifetime in only receiving a seven-year sentence," he prodded. Sophie held her ground, explaining that she wanted to accept responsibility for her role in the murders. I was quite surprised how she was able to answer Ed's questions and deflect the answers away from herself and back toward Angelo. I had to give her credit; Ed couldn't get her to change her testimony at all. She held firm to her assertion that Angelo was responsible and she articulated all her answers clearly.

Lloyd didn't want to cross examine and he looked relieved when Sophie got off the stand. I looked across the courtroom at Angelo; he was looking at the ground and uttering something like, 'no, no, she is lying'.

Prosecuting Attorney Lloyd Fox stated to the judge that the Crown's case was now complete and no more witnesses would be called. The judge asked Attorney Ed Williams if he was prepared to start his defense argument, and how many witnesses he expected to call to testify.

"I'll only be calling two witnesses," he said. His first witness would be Dr. Goldstein, an expert witness in the field of psychiatry. His second witness would be Angelo. "However, I'm going to file a number of documents with the court," he said. Then he gave the court clerk a stack of documents for the judge and he gave the prosecutor a similar stack. Court was adjourned for the day and was scheduled to start at ten the next morning.

I met Stephanie and Corey in the hallway and we started walking back to the police station. I noticed a bar and asked them if they had time for a quick drink. They both said, "Yes." After listening to Sophie's testimony, everybody needed one.

We found a quiet table in the back of the bar and started talking about what Sophie had said on the stand. "She did a good job testifying," said Corey.

I chuckled and said, "How many weeks did Lloyd's team

coach her?" They both shook their heads at me. I said, "Hold on, listen to me for a minute. Did Sophie really strike you as a typical domestic abuse victim? I don't think so. At times in her testimony she spoke with a hint of arrogance. She's a controller. She tried to look everyone in the eye when she spoke, so the whole courtroom understood that she was in control. That is *not* how victims of domestic violence act."

"Maybe it has to do with her heritage and background," suggested Stephanie. "Some Italian women run the household."

I said, "Okay, let's agree to disagree." Corey didn't say anything.

We had two quick drinks and left. I told them that I would see Doctor Goldstein and Angelo testify, and that would be it. "The days are too long for me, travelling down to Bisson City, sitting in court all day and then driving back home. I'm not feeling that good these days." Then I shook Corey's hand, hugged Stephanie and I left. Of course it was a long drive home and I was stuck in rush hour traffic.

When I got home, Karen had already made dinner. As we ate, I gave Karen an update on Sophie's testimony. She said she'd seen the six o'clock news and the reporter had said exactly what I'd said. After dinner, I was really tied so I went to bed at eight o'clock. When I woke in the morning, I felt terrible. I was stiff all over and short of breath. I told Karen I wouldn't be going to court. "Good," she said. "Get some rest."

I phoned Stephanie and told her I didn't feel up to going to court and asked her to call me after court and give me an update. In a motherly tone, Stephanie said, "Alex, you look after yourself. I'm really concerned about you. Get some rest. Don't worry about court. The case will be in the jury's hands soon, and it's up to them to render a verdict."

I took it easy all day and just lay on the couch most of the time, watching television. I slept on and off and I started to feel better. My cell phone rang around five o'clock. It was Stephanie, who said she'd just gotten home and poured herself a glass of wine. She asked how I felt, then she told me about court.

"The court declared Dr. Goldstein as an expert witness in the field of psychiatry. Both Angelo and Sophie consented to psychiatric testing and he was the one who tested them. He described Angelo as being a little delayed mentally. He said his educational records indicated that hadn't completed high school, thought he didn't say why. He also said that a number of psychological tests conducted on Angelo indicated that Angelo has a mild form of psychotic anger disorder. Basically, he explodes into a fits of anger if he didn't take his mediation on a daily basis."

"Not too surprising," I said.

She continued, "Dr. Goldstein obtained Angelo's medical records from his family doctor, who has been prescribing medication to Angelo for the last 25 years. Dr. Goldstein said Angelo had been ordering and picking up his medication on a regular basis and appeared to be taking it as prescribed. Then he talked about Sophie and said all his tests on *her* indicated she had a dissociative disorder, or possibly a multiple personality disorder."

"Now that's more like it," I said. "I'm with the good doctor on that."

"It's another sad victim story, I guess," said Stephanie with a sigh. "Dr. Goldstein said Sophie was exposed to severe trauma as a child. She was repetitively physically and mentally abused by her parents, who ran a very disciplined household. If she was caught doing anything wrong she was severely punished. He also said that neighbor sexually assaulted her when she was about 12. She told her parents about the sexual assault and Sophie's father spoke to the neighbour's son, who had assaulted her. Then, because both families had some type of family honor code, they agreed not to report the incident to the police. He said he'd need to do further testing on her, but his preliminary finding was that one of Sophie's personality disorders was that she needed absolute control over situations and had to be in a position of power, exhibiting dominance. He said at times she could also exhibit predatory behaviours."

I asked Stephanie, "What did you think of the doctor's testimony?"

She said, "He gave great testimony and some of his evidence silenced the court."

I said, "It's about time some evidence against Sophie came out."

"Agreed," said Stephanie. Then she said, "Angelo is scheduled to testify tomorrow. Are you going to go to court?"

I said, "Yes."

Then Stephanie said she had something else to tell me. "I've been thinking a lot about what my life priorities are. I have fond memories and feelings about lying next to you in my bed. It was so nice, and I want to have someone in my life that I can share the same feelings with. When this trial is over, I'm going to take your advice and ask for a transfer out of the homicide unit."

I told her, "That's a good idea. You need a break from the stress."

"And I have one more thing to tell you," she said. "I met someone."

I said, "Please, tell all!"

She said, "I went out with Corey on a couple of dates."

I said, "Stephanie, you're about 42 and what's he, about 35?"

She said, "So what's wrong with a girl having a boy toy and having some fun?"

I laughed and said, "That's good for you—and Corey."

"We're keeping our relationship quiet at work. It's only been a couple of dates so far, and we haven't slept together yet. We're taking it slow, but tonight is the third date so it's probably going to happen. I have urges that need to be fulfilled."

I said, "That's good. I hope he can fulfill all your urges." We both laughed and then Stephanie said she would meet me in the lobby of the police station at around eight-thirty the next morning.

I got up and was down at the police station bright and early. Corey and Stephanie met me in the lobby. I shook Corey's hand and gave Stephanie a hug. She whispered in my ear that her urges had been fulfilled last night. I whispered back, "You better wipe that 'I just got fucked' look off your face before someone figures out what's going on."

Stephanie said, "Oh Alex, stop it!" and slapped me on the shoulder.

Corey asked, "What's going on?"

I leaned over and whispered in his ear, "I know what's going on and you better treat that girl good or you will have to deal with me."

Corey loudly asked, "You know what's going on?"

I said, "Of course I do. I'm an old, retired cop."

We walked up the street together to the court house. Stephanie and Corey both seemed happier and I was thinking, *of course they do.* They were probably like a couple of horny rabbits all night long and I would bet that neither one of them slept much. I was actually pretty happy for both of them.

When we got to court, as usual, Stephanie and Corey went off to the prosecutor's office while I waited in the hallway for court to start. I was anxious to hear what Angelo had to say. When it was announced that court was about to start, I went into the room and found a seat. Angelo was brought into the courtroom and placed at the table with his lawyer. We all stood when the jury and judge came in.

Angelo's name was called by the court clerk to take the stand and he was sworn in. He sat in the witness box and his attorney, Ed, started with some basic questions, which Angelo answered. When he spoke, he didn't appear to be that confident. After a while, Ed told the court he wanted to play Angelo's video statement from his arrest. I thought, *if a person is arrested for seven murders why would he give a statement to police before talking to his lawyer?* Just looking at Angelo, I could tell there was something cowed about his persona. Unlike his wife , he appeared very timid. My thoughts about Sophie's guilt grew stronger.

Angelo's recorded statement was similar to Sophie's, right up to the point where he started talking about *Sophie* being a mean, abusive drunk. He said Sophie hadn't been interested in sex for nearly 20 years and they had separate bedrooms. He said he slept on the cot in the basement while Sophie slept in the upstairs bedroom on the second floor. Other than sleeping on different floors, they shared the rest of the house. Then he stated that when Sophie got drunk, sometimes she came down to the basement and beat him.

One night, she came down the basement stairs with a rolling pin to hit him, something she'd done in the past. She was drunk and angry and so she missed the last few stairs and fell. She hit her head on the floor and passed out, and that's when he decided he was going to do something to stop the beatings. He got a chain out of the garage, attached it to a metal support pole for the house and, using a pair of handcuffs left behind by the escort, handcuffed her to it. He made her stay there for a day until she promised she would never hit him again. He said that was the last time Sophie actually hit him.

Then he talked about the hooker he'd had sex with, the 'mistake' he'd made, which was another common thread in their two stories. His version was that one night, when Sophie was at the local bar drinking, he invited a hooker who'd once given him a blow job to the house for sex. He said he thought her name was Sunshine. Since Sophie's bedroom was nicer, and she was out at the bar, he took Sunshine up to Sophie's room. Unfortunately, Sophie came home early and caught them having at it in her bed. Angelo said she freaked, dragged Sunshine out of the bedroom and threw her down the stairs, calling her 'slut' and every other name she could think of. Then she continued beating her up and dragged her outside. At point, Angelo said he was so frightened that he ran down to the basement, locked the door and hid in his bed. He was not sure what happened to Sunshine, but after that incident, Sophie got even meaner. She swore at him all the time and made comments about him fucking prostitutes.

Angelo further stated in his taped interview that a few nights later they loaded the hot dog cart into their van, which was parked in a laneway. Sophie observed a blonde girl passed out in the laneway near where they parked the van and she just grabbed a plastic bag from the van, ran over to the woman and put the plastic bag over the girl's head and held it there until she stopped moving. On the recording, Angelo was now crying.

He went on to tell the police that she then grabbed a metal rod from the van, went over to the girl and pulled her panties down. He said Sophie rammed the metal rod into the girl's vagina while calling her a slut and muttering, 'how dare you sleep in my bed and have sex with my husband'. Sophie eventually stopped the assault and ordered him to help her move the body, or she would tell the police that *he* did that stuff to the girl.

During the rest of the recorded interview, he explained to the police how all the other girls were killed. He said once Sophie went into a fit of rage when she discovered that one girl was actually a guy. She got the knife from their van and cut the guy up bad. For the rest of the interview, Angelo basically said he couldn't control or stop Sophie, that he was scared of her and he decided to just help her. Although Sophie was killing the girls, at least she wasn't beating him up or hurting *him* anymore.

After listening to Angelo's horrendous, graphic recorded statement, sobs could be heard throughout the courtroom. The judge suggested to Ed that it would probably be a good time for the morning break. He further said they would add the morning break to the lunch break, since Angelo's recorded interview had been so long.

I knew the police had briefed the victims' families about the graphic testimony they were going to hear, but still, my heart went out to them. I saw Sally Armstrong's mother crying as she came out of court.

I met Corey and Stephanie in the hallway. "Angelo's original interview is pretty compelling," I said.

Stephanie said, "We've been struggling with the same issue. Both Angelo's and Sophie's testimonies are compelling."

Court was called to session after the lunch break. Angelo returned to the witness box and continued his testimony and Ed spent the rest of the afternoon asking Angelo clarifying questions about his original statement to police. Although the judge had to ask Angelo several times to speak up, I thought he did a reasonable job testifying. Angelo finished giving his evidence at the end of the day. Now it was Lloyd's turn to cross examine, but court was finishing for the day, adjourned to Monday morning.

Once again, I walked back to the police station with Stephanie and Corey. On the way, I asked Stephanie if she had any more information on Sunshine. Stephanie said, "We heard Sunshine might have moved to the Windsor area to work as an escort."

I asked, "Did anyone from forensics have any luck in developing a DNA match for the blood found near the Martinos' front door?"

Stephanie said, "We got some help from United States' advanced DNA profiling center and they confirmed the DNA came from a female, and that the female was probably Caucasian."

Corey said, "We ran the DNA profile through the national DNA data bank again, but there were still no matching profiles. I'm sure you already know that not everyone's DNA is in the system."

I told both of them, "I know a deal has already been made with Sophie, but it would be nice to track down this Sunshine girl and find out the truth about which Martino beat her up. That would certainly add credibility to one of the Martinos' versions of events."

"I know," said Stephanie, "We've tried to find out who she is and the investigative team spent a lot of time trying to track her down. But without a proper name, it's been no dice. We sent two detectives to the Windsor area and they worked the streets with Windsor Vice, but no luck. It's possible Sunshine could have changed her street name."

As we said good bye, I told Stephanie, "I have to work Sunday night, but I am still planning to attend court Monday morning. Could I have a shower and a coffee at your place so I don't have to drive home in between?"

"Sure," she said. Then she added, "There's a good chance Corey will be there too."

I asked, "Would it be okay if I came by around 6:45 in the morning? I'll text first because so I don't interrupt any morning activities." She laughed.

I got home late because of rush hour traffic to find Karen already home and making dinner. "Hi," I said.

"Hi yourself," she said. "I hope you feel like pasta tonight."

"I feel like whatever you're making," I said. Then I told Karen my thoughts on Angelo's testimony and about the missing escort, Sunshine. Karen said, "It sounds like they made the deal with the wrong person."

I agreed. "They're both guilty and deserve to be convicted on all seven homicides, but if they had to make a deal with anyone, they sure as hell *did* make a deal with the wrong person."

Karen and I didn't do too much on the weekend. Mostly we hung out in the yard and relaxed watching TV. Soon it was Sunday night and time for me to do my weekly shift, plus I was going to change at Stephanie's for court. I grabbed my usual work stuff and a suit for court. I almost forgot to bring a tie and a pair of shoes, but remembered at the last minute.

I drove downtown to Featherstone's truck compound and fired up the garbage truck. As I set out on my route, I thought about Sunshine. I wondered if Sophie had killed her. If a woman with a mental health problem catches her spouse with a hooker in her bed that could send her into homicidal rage. I also thought about how its been demonstrated time and time again how most serial killers progress in their criminal behaviour. Lots of them abuse and torture animals to start. I wondered if Sophie was like that. From what I'd heard, he had no remorse for some brutal assaults on Angelo. Once she killed one hooker, how big of a sociopathic leap was it to kill another ... and another. Then I wondered why she'd suffocated them with plastic bags. Was it the closest tool? Or did she want to look into their eyes when she killed them?

If Angelo was truly the aggressor, as Sophie stated, he could just as easily have killed Sunshine. But I was pretty sure he wasn't—and I also believed there was enough evidence to support my theory. I wondered about the area *around* the Martino house. Was the house and yard laid out in a way that a body could be buried? I'd seen pictures of it on the news, but hadn't been able to tell. I decided I would drive by and take a look at it. It was in the west end of the city, not too far away from the dump.

The truck is large and it makes a lot of noise, so to avoid waking up a residential neighbourhood, I decided to park it at a plaza down the street and walk to the Martino home. I got out of the truck and slowly walked down DuPont Street until I found the house. It was a bungalow, with a half-storey second floor. A small, partially dissembled front porch was attached to the house. I wondered if the police had ripped it apart looking for evidence, but then I thought that it's possible it was just like that. It didn't look like anyone had looked after the house since the Martinos got thrown in jail.

There was one thing unusual about the Martinos' house that I noticed right away, While one side of the house was about 15 feet away from the neighbours, the other had a narrow driveway that led to the rear of the house. It was unusual to have a driveway in that neighbourhood, and most of the homes did not.

There is usually a laneway running behind most houses in Bisson City, and residents' garages generally back onto it. I decided to walk around the corner and look for the laneway. Shortly, I found the back of the Martino residence and I noticed they did not have a garage at the rear of their property, just an old-style, six-foot-high fence. I looked over the fence and into their yard. It was cluttered with junk, and there were also a couple of out-buildings in it. I presumed the larger building that was half-way down their long, narrow lot was a garage, while and the two other buildings beside an uncared-for garden were sheds.

I didn't see anything too unusual, but I wasn't sure if the police had searched the outside buildings. Most likely they had.

I walked back to the truck and finished my shift and then I dropped off the garbage truck and I drove to Stephanie's condo. It was only 6:15 so I waited five minutes and then texted Stephanie. She texted me back and said it was good timing and to come up. I grabbed my change of clothing and buzzed her. She let me in.

As I rode up the elevator, I thought, *Corey is probably there and they probably fucked all weekend long, like every new couple in a hot and heavy relationship.* I was kind of jealous.

Stephanie opened the door. She was dressed for work and she said, "I made coffee and eggs." Then she gave me a hug, wrinkled her nose and told me to take a shower. I guessed I smelled like garbage and sweat.

She walked me to the spare bathroom and handed me a towel. I saw Corey in the main bathroom. He wasn't wearing a shirt. Corey had a good, lean muscular build that I was sure Stephanie liked.

I showered and put my suit on and then met both of them at the kitchen island. I shook Corey's hand when I saw him and asked how their weekend was.

Corey said, "We had a quiet weekend and just hung around Stephanie's place most of time."

I poured myself a coffee and grabbed some scrambled eggs and then I asked if they had even left the condo. Stephanie giggled and said, "Yes, we left." Corey just raised an eyebrow at me, indicating that it was none of my business.

I said, "I know it's early, but I need to ask a question about the Martino house."

Corey said, "Ask away."

I said, "I've been thinking about Sunshine's disappearance. Do you think it's possible that one of the Martinos killed Sunshine and buried her in the back yard?"

Stephanie said, "Well, that was not one of the original investigative concerns when we executed the search warrant, so no. We had no evidence to suggest Sunshine might have been murdered and buried on the property so we weren't looking for a body."

"Well, with all the time that's passed, you're in a good position to apply for another search warrant. I think you should."

"Executing another warrant on the Martino property might affect the trial," said Stephanie. "Maybe it should wait until the trial is over so we don't compromise it."

Corey said, "I actually proposed that idea to the prosecutor already, but he told me to hold off."

Stephanie looked at her watch and said, "We better get going or we're going to be late." I left my truck at Stephanie's, as she only lives ten minutes away from the police station, and she drove us all to the police station. From there we walked to the courthouse and while they went to see Lloyd and Samantha to discuss Lloyd's cross examination of Angelo, I waited in the hallway outside the courtroom. I people-watched and I recognised a number of regular faces. I saw Mr. and Mrs. Armstrong and said good morning to them. I also recognised the St. Cyr family as they were walking down the hallway.

I thought, *how terrible it must be for the victims' families to have to spend weeks and weeks in court.* Most of them probably had to rent hotel rooms during the week, and for what? To obtain a better understanding on how their poor children had been murdered? Would it bring closure? I doubted it. I knew there was never closure when a loved one was senselessly murdered. You can never forget a child you've lost.

Soon Lloyd, Samantha, Stephanie and Corey went into the courtroom and I went into it after them. As I sat down, I saw the court officers bringing Angelo in from the secured prisoner passageway.

As soon as the judge and jury arrived, court started. Angelo was called to return to stand and Lloyd began the cross examination. As had happened with Sophie on cross, Angelo never swayed from his original evidence and he did a pretty good job on the stand. I was certain some of the jury members were considering Angelo's version of the events. After several hours, Angelo was released from the stand and Ed said he had finished calling witnesses.

Court ended early, at one o'clock, and I couldn't have been happier about it. I was exhausted from not sleeping and I had that blurred, tired vision thing starting. The judge looked at both attorneys and said, "Closing arguments will start on Tuesday and I'm expecting to give my charge to the members of the jury on Wednesday." And with that, everyone left.

I walked back down to the police station with Stephanie and Corey. "I have no interest in hearing the closing arguments," I said. "How about you guys just give me periodic updates on how the trial is going?"

"No problem, Alex," said Stephanie.

Corey stayed at the police station and Stephanie drove me back to my pickup truck. On the way back to the truck I asked Stephanie, "How is it going with Corey?"

She said, "It's only been a month or so, but things are really good."

"I'm happy for both of you," I said.

"Corey told me about what you said to him about not ever hurting me," she said. "Alex, I think you might have scared him."

"I hope nobody ever hurts one my friends, Stephanie," I said.

"Thanks, Alex," she said and then she gave me a hug and a kiss on the cheek.

It was a tough drive up the highway to my home. I could hardly keep my eyes open. When I got home, I went right to bed. I woke up a few hours later when Karen came home. I wasn't feeling that good. I had a bit to eat and told Karen I was too tired to stay up. It was only 7:30, but I went to bed for the night.

Stephanie was good for her word about calling. I heard from her the next evening about the closing arguments. It went as expected. She also told me she'd gotten funding approval to execute a search warrant on the Martino property. She said they would try to obtain the warrant after the jury came in with a verdict.

"We're going to bring in an expensive ground penetrating radar machine and also some cadaver dogs," she said. I asked if she thought Angelo would get convicted or not. "He and his defence team put up a good argument, but I'd be surprised if he didn't," she said.

I replied, "Unfortunately, I think you're right."

"Corey and I are starting to think that maybe you're right ... maybe she's the aggressor and the prosecutor made a mistake in rushing into a deal with her. We tried to discuss our concerns with Lloyd and Samantha, but they shot the idea down. They said, 'let the jury make their decision'."

The next day the judge made his charge to the jury and sent them to make their decision. I figured the jury would only take two days or so, as they probably didn't want to spend any more time sequestered away from their families.

Sure enough, late Friday afternoon Stephanie phoned me to say the jury had found Angelo guilty of five counts of first-degree murder and two counts of second-degree murder. "The court erupted into applause when the head juror read the verdict. The judge said he supported the jury's decision and scheduled sentencing arguments for the following week."

"How many life sentences can a man really serve?" I asked. "He's not going to see daylight again, so it doesn't matter how many he got handed, does it?" Then I said, "By the way, congratulations on leading a successful investigation and getting a conviction. Make sure you tell Corey he did a good job too."

"Thanks, Alex," said Stephanie.

That night, I watched the six o'clock news on television. Angelo's conviction was on every news station. I thought that it was funny that everybody—the mayor, police chief and a variety of politicians—were patting each other on the back. The only people who thanked the homicide team for all their hard work and dedication were the victims' families.

The following week Stephanie called me to tell me that Angelo got sentenced to seven life sentences.

"Well, I guess he deserved it, but so does Sophie," I said grouchily. "I'm still not happy with her deal, but at least one of them is getting punished."

"Agreed," said Stephanie. "But if it makes you feel any better, we got a search warrant and will execute it on Tuesday. If you want to come to the scene with me and watch from a distance, you can."

"You bet. Where should I meet you?"

"We're going to meet at a plaza near the Martinos' house around 9:30 a.m."

"I'll see you there," I said.

CHAPTER 12

The weekend passed by pretty quickly. I worked my Sunday night shift without any problems, though I was extra tired throughout the shift. I wondered if the heart medication was making me feel drowsy.

I slept through most of Monday and then got up and had dinner with Karen. I told her Stephanie and Corey were dating and she said she was happy Stephanie had found someone. However, I knew she wasn't happy with the fact that I was going down to Bisson City to watch the police execute their search warrant on the Martino property. I told her, "I'm not going to stay that long. I will see you when you get home."

She reminded me, "Whatever you do, Alex, don't get too excited. Try to remain calm."

I left the house a little later than usual and got stuck in the early morning rush hour. It was slow going, but I wasn't too stressed as I'd allowed some extra time. I arrived at the plaza on DuPont Street just before nine-thirty. A large section of the parking lot was taped off for police vehicles, and there was a briefing area set up. I parked and walked over to the police tape and then stood there hoping Stephanie or Corey would notice me.

In the distance I saw Stephanie briefing a number of police officers. I stood there watching until I heard Corey's voice. "Good morning, Alex," he said. We shook hands and he told me I could observe what was going on, but I had to stay with him or Stephanie at all times. "Even though Angelo's been convicted, this is still a criminal investigation and that's why we have to restrict your involvement."

"I understand," I said.

As we stood around waiting for things to start happening, I asked, "How's it going with Stephanie?"

He beamed as he said, "It's going great. It's a little awkward, since she's my boss. We have to be careful in the office."

"I'm glad to hear it," I told him, "She's a good person." Then I said, "Tell me about the execution of the search warrant."

He said, "Well, the house is still vacant so we're going to place one uniformed officer at the front and one at the rear of the residence and then tape a copy of the search warrant to the front door. We've arranged for copies of the search warrant to be delivered to both Angelo and Sophie. The warrant is only for searching the exterior property of the house and the interior of the outside buildings."

"Probably that's all you're going to need. Do you expect to find a body?" I asked.

Corey said, "We arranged for a forensic anthropologist to be on standby just in case we do. Stephanie's plan is to have a cadaver dog go over the property and check inside the buildings. Then, depending on results, we'll use the ground penetrating radar to go over the property. If that shows anything, we'll mark any interesting areas and then carefully dig them up."

During my police career, I had the opportunity to use cadaver dogs in a couple of investigations. Most of the time the dog handler and dog were successful in locating the bodies of the missing victims. They're very accurate. There are a few variables that can throw a dog off, like soil type and terrain, but I was pretty sure the dog wouldn't have any issues with the Martino property. For a moment, I thought of Kobe and his great nose. That dog would never miss a rabbit scent. It was ironic that it was his nose that killed him.

I saw Stephanie walking toward us. When she arrived, she said the entry team would execute the warrant in a few minutes and the property would be secured shortly after that. Then the three of us walked down the street toward the Martino house. Across the street, I saw three police cars pull up. The officers got out of the cars and quickly secured the area around the house with police tape. A couple of detectives went to the door and knocked. When there was no response, they stuck a copy of the search warrant on the front door.

Stephanie, Corey and I stood across the street and watched the police officers work. They quickly checked the interior of all the outside buildings and then one officer took a position at the rear of the residence and the other took a position at the front, as planned.

Stephanie said to me, "The K-9 unit will be arriving soon." Sure enough, a few minutes later a marked vehicle with 'K-9' written on the side of it pulled up to the front of the house. A police officer wearing tactical clothing exited the vehicle, opened the rear door, leashed the occupant of the back seat and then removed the dog from the vehicle. The dog appeared to be a black Labrador retriever. Except for the colour, he looked just like Kobe.

The dog wasted no time; as soon as the handler got near the house, it started pulling hard towards the garage, literally dragging the handler. Then, just inside the garage door, it stopped, sat down and looked at the ground.

Both Stephanie and Corey said at the same time, "It's onto something."

I said, "Well that was fast."

The dog had clearly smelled something strong. The handler yelled, "Inspector Foster! I think the dog has found something."

Stephanie told the dog handler, "Check the other buildings," but the dog kept pulling the handler back towards the garage.

Then Stephanie and Corey started making phone calls. "We're going to set up an inner perimeter around the garage and make arrangements for the forensic unit and the anthropologist to check things out," she said to me by way of explanation.

When I had a chance, I interrupted Stephanie and said, "I think there's a good chance you have your missing person. I know you and Corey are both going to be very busy now, so I'm going home. Give me an update when you have a chance."

Stephanie said, "Okay, Alex. And thanks for coming." Then she got back to work. It would take days to process the ground inside the garage, and if Sunshine's remains were buried there, it could even take longer.

I got home just after lunch and lay down for a quick afternoon nap, waking up just in time to watch the six o'clock news. Sure enough, the top story on the news was that the police had obtained another search warrant for the Martino house. This time I listened to Corey being interviewed. He said police had obtained and executed a search warrant at the residence and that they were in the preliminary stages of another investigation related to the Martinos. He appeared very professional during his interview.

I was pretty sure they had found human remains, probably Sunshine's, and I hoped they found enough evidence to charge Sophie and Angelo both. I believed Angelo's story and I was convinced that Sophie had murdered Sunshine in a fit of rage. I hoped the police would obtain evidence at the scene to properly identify Sunshine. Someone out there probably wanted to know what happened to her. She'd been missing for almost four years.

I didn't do too much for the next couple of days. I had some more tests at Dr. Burns' office and things hadn't changed much with my heart. I got the same speech about taking it easy and calling an ambulance right away if I thought I was having a heart attack.

Later that evening, I got a phone call from Stephanie. "Skeletal remains were found under the gravel floor of the garage," she said. "Everyone is taking their time processing the scene. The forensic anthropologists said the bones were definitely human, probably female, and that they had a lot of fractures. We also found some clothing and a cell phone buried near the victim. And it seems someone poured a large amount of bleach over the victim's body."

I asked Stephanie, "Will the phone be examined? Maybe it will provide some evidence."

She said, "It's with the electronic crimes technological unit as we speak."

"Great," I said, then I asked, "And how are *you* doing?"

"Processing the scene is slow but we're stopping work when it gets dark, so I've been able to get home at a reasonable time and get a good night's sleep."

"That's good," I said. "And what's next?"

She said, "The victim's body will probably be removed from the scene tomorrow and then we'll process the rest of the property."

I told her to call with any updates. She said she would and was about to go when I asked, "How are you *really* doing? How are you and Corey doing?"

Stephanie hesitated a few seconds and said, "Well, it's good with Corey, but the job is getting to me again. I met with my boss and requested a transferred. I guess I've finally realized there is more to life than working. I've spent my life climbing the ladder in the homicide unit, and my personal life seems to have passed me by. At one time, I wanted to have children and to move out of the city to the country. If I don't start pursuing that now, I'll miss the boat. So, I still want to be a cop ... but I need to scale it back a notch. I still love working in the homicide unit and investigating homicides, but the adrenaline rush of conducting murder investigations has taken over my life and I need it back now."

"Well it would seem that maybe *now* is a good time to catch up on your personal life. It sounds like things are moving along really great with Corey. Maybe he's the one, the one who can be your soul mate and partner. You could still have children, or at least you could adopt some."

"Hey, Alex, slow down a bit," Stephanie said.

I said, "No, do what you have to do to be happy—you deserve it."

"Thanks for speaking honestly, Alex," Stephanie said softly. Then she said she'd give me updates on the investigation into Sunshine's identity.

Later that night, I got a phone call from Allan Featherstone. He asked how I was doing, and I said 'okay'. He said, "We had to let one of the night drivers go. I was wondering if you felt up to working a few extra night shifts until I find another driver?"

I said, "I can probably work the Sunday to Thursday shift, but only for a few weeks."

"How about a day shift, Monday to Thursday, starting at 7:00 a.m. and ending at 3:00 p.m.?

I said, "Thanks, but no thanks. The traffic downtown is absolutely terrible during the day."

He laughed. It was true. Then he asked, "Can you start this Sunday night and work to Thursday night?

Reluctantly, I said, "Okay."

Karen came home and over dinner I told her about Allan's phone call. She said, "You shouldn't be working at all, never mind more hours." I promised her it would be just for a few weeks. Then I told Karen about the conversation I'd had with Stephanie. "Although Stephanie likes working in the homicide unit, she feels like she's got her life priorities all mixed up. She thinks she's been over-committed to her job and that her personal life has slipped away from her."

"Did the conversation with Stephanie sound familiar?" Karen asked.

I thought for a few seconds and then said, "Yes, it did."

"You were the same as Stephanie," Karen said, "At times you were a workaholic. It's no secret to either of us that you put that job before me and the kids."

"I know," I said. Then I walked over to her, bent down and

gave her a kiss on the cheek. "Thank you for standing by me and supporting me over the years," I said. Then I offered to take her upstairs and show her my appreciation, but she said, "No, that's okay. My television show is about to start. Maybe later."

I thought, *oh well, at least I got her to smile.*

I started working my four night shifts a week and I didn't hear anything from Stephanie for the next week or so. After my last shift, I phoned Allan and asked him if he had hired another driver yet. He said, "I hired a driver, but the new guy can't start for another week."

"I said, "Allan, listen, I can only do one more four-nighter for you, and that's it. This schedule is really starting to bother me. I think I must be getting old."

"Can you still work one Sunday shift a week?" he asked.

"Probably for another couple of months," I said. And finally I admitted, "I really want to stop working."

Allan said, "Well, it's time, old buddy. Thanks, thought. I appreciate you working these extra hours for me."

Later in the afternoon, Stephanie called and said they were having difficulty figuring out who Sunshine actually was. She asked me if we could meet and discuss it.

"I'm working some extra shifts, so I can meet you at a coffee shop before, during or after my shift, or else you will have to wait until Friday."

Stephanie said, "I've taken Thursday and Friday off. Why don't we do breakfast together early Thursday morning."

"Let's meet at a place I know just north of Bisson City called the Northern Star Bar and Grill."

Stephanie said, "Sure, I will see you there around seven for breakfast."

I hadn't seen Stephanie for a few weeks and looked forward to seeing her. I wasn't sure if she was going to bring Corey or not, but it didn't matter. Although I didn't get a great first impression from Corey, now that I knew him better, he was growing on me.

He certainly made Stephanie feel good and she seemed happy with him.

As I worked my last night of the four-nighter for Allan, I realized nothing much had changed in downtown Bisson City among the night people. Even the prostitutes hadn't changed. It was the same girls working the same nights. I was happy this was my last shift. I would be meeting Stephanie in a few hours so I had a change of clothes with me. I didn't want to smell of garbage while I was having breakfast with her.

I dropped the garbage truck off at the compound and changed in the washroom and then drove my pickup truck up to the restaurant. I met Stephanie in the parking lot as she was exiting her car. She was by herself and was dressed casually, in jeans. We gave each other a hug and walked into the restaurant together.

We sat down, ordered coffees and asked for a menu. Stephanie said, "Corey had to work and my supervisor told me to start burning off some accumulated time, so I took a couple of days off."

I asked her how she was doing and she said fine. She asked, "How is the old ticker?"

"The old ticker acts up off and on, and I might be having another by-pass surgery in a couple of months," I told her. "Also, I'm getting burned out working the midnight shifts and I am thinking about quitting my job in a few months."

"Good. You have to take it easy, Alex," Stephanie said. Then she asked, "So what do you want to talk about first, the Sunshine homicide investigation or how Corey and I are doing?"

I said, "Let's talk about something cheerful. How are things with Corey?"

Stephanie smiled and said, "Simply amazing. So good that he took me to meet his parents and we had dinner with them. They seem like really nice people and Corey's mother pulled me aside and told me that I must be very special, as Corey rarely brings any of his girlfriends home to meet them."

I told Stephanie, "That's great."

Stephanie then said, "Of course they brought out the family pictures, and showed me pictures of Corey when he was a baby."

I said, "Wow, things are moving along nicely."

Stephanie said, "We also talked about moving in together. His apartment lease is expiring, and since we spend so much time together, we thought he could move into my place."

I told Stephanie, "I'm happy to hear how your relationship is developing."

Peggy, our waitress, came by and we ordered breakfast. Surprisingly, Stephanie ordered the king size breakfast, while I just ordered toast and eggs. I jokingly told her she must be burning off a lot of calories with Corey to be ordering a breakfast that size. She just laughed. "Guess what?" she asked.

"What?" I said.

"My transfer has been approved and I'm going back to uniform duties as an inspector in the east end division in about six months. I also made the short list for the rank of superintendent."

"Wow, that's great," I said. I certainly believed she deserved a promotion based on her hard work and dedication.

"Once I get transferred, Corey and I will be finally be able to be a couple in public. We hide it at work right now."

"Good idea," I said, then I asked, "And how is the Sunshine murder investigation going? Any new evidence?"

"We've had no success identifying her yet but the coroner said the cause of death was homicide, blunt force trauma. There were numerous crushed and broken bones consistent with being struck with a heavy tool, like a hammer or a sledge hammer. Police seized all the tools in the garage and forensic testing matched Sunshine's DNA to the DNA on a shovel and ball peen hammer."

"I just know it was Sophie," I said.

"We sent police officers to re-interview both Sophie and Angelo about Sunshine's body being in their garage. They both consented, but asked to have their lawyers present during their interviews."

"So what did they say?" I asked Stephanie.

"It was classic," she sighed. "They repeated exactly what they said on the stand and in their police interviews. They blamed each other for Sunshine's murder. Sophie said she never went to the backyard or garage, as that was Angelo's shop area. She went into great detail about how Angelo often worked in the garage at strange times and he spent a lot of time working in his garden."

"And what did Angelo say?"

"Angelo said he never noticed anything unusual in the garage, except once raccoons or squirrels got into it and spilled a bunch of his gardening chemicals all over his work bench and the garage floor. He said the chemicals eventually soaked into the gravel floor of the garage. He couldn't remember what specific chemicals had spilled, but they all were for gardening and weed control."

"Of course. Blame the squirrels," I said drily. "Now what?" I asked.

"The investigative team is meeting with the prosecutor. The prosecutor's office said there is a lot of circumstantial evidence against the Martinos, but they need some direct evidence to lay another criminal charge. One assistant prosecutor joked about spending time and money to prosecute someone who's already serving seven life sentences. But if we could prove Sophie was responsible Sunshine's death,that would be sure change things. But we need more direct evidence."

"So what investigative steps are being taken to identify Sunshine?" I asked.

"We're working on a couple of different angles. We're working with a forensic artist to make a clay model of Sunshine's face, based on the shape of her skull, then we're going to post her picture and see if anyone recognizes her. We know she's a blonde, but that's all we know at this point."

"What about the phone?" I asked.

"Unfortunately, the sim card was too damaged to get any information from it and circling back to the escort service she worked for also turned up nothing. It's really frustrating. Do you have any good ideas?"

I said, "Not really. But sometimes you have to consider asking a different type of investigative question to get answers."

Stephanie said, "What do you mean?"

I said, "No offence to the officers you originally sent to the escort service, but did they ask the right people the right questions?"

Stephanie asked, "Alex, what the hell are you talking about?"

I said, "In a three- to five-year period, how many different escorts do you think would have been employed at that place? How long has the joint been in business? How many different owners or managers has there been? Different owners may keep different filing systems on their employees and clients. Do you see what I'm getting at?"

She nodded.

"Like every business, employees come and go. *Someone* remembers her. Maybe an ex-employee, maybe someone who used to own the business and hired her. Maybe a regular client of hers. You have to consider sending back some different detectives, probably a female and male team. Have them dig into the business records going back at least six months before Sunshine even started working there. A female cop should be able to build a better rapport with a male. If you find some of Sunshine's co-workers from when she was employed there, maybe one of them will have some information on her."

Stephanie agreed that perhaps the original investigators hadn't dug deep enough into the escort business angle. "I'll get a couple more investigators to go back there," she said, "And yes, one will be a female."

I glanced at the clock on the restaurant's wall and couldn't believe that two hours had already passed. We'd had three coffees each and we decided we needed a washroom break. When we returned, I asked what Stephanie had planned for the rest of the day. "Not too much," she said.

I asked, "Do you want to go for a walk and finish our discussion?"

She said, "Sure."

I paid our bill and we decided to go for just a short walk, only 30 minutes, to burn off our breakfasts. While we were walking, Stephanie said she'd forgotten to tell me a couple of things. "Angelo and Sophie had their lawyers sell their house for them. Apparently it went quickly and they already split up the money. And Angelo is filing a motion to appeal his murder convictions. But the prosecutor's office hasn't told me what they are actually appealing."

"I'm not surprised," I said. "Angelo has nothing to lose by filing an appeal. If Angelo's lawyer find grounds, like some error in law or abuse of process, why not? It might get him a retrial. But it sure would be hard on the families of those girls. If you ask me, I think they should both be locked up for the rest of their lives."

"I have one more thing to share," she said. "I know you are going to be pretty pissed off about this, but I wanted to tell you before you heard it from another source."

I said, "What is it?"

"Some women's rights groups have been petitioning for an early parole hearing and release date for Sophie."

I asked Stephanie, "How is it even possible for her to get an early release? She's only been in custody since her arrest two years ago! I can't believe how someone pleads guilty, gets a seven-year sentence and is paroled after serving less than three years!"

"It depends on her parole eligibility date, you know that. Most inmates are eligible for parole after serving one-third of their sentence. In fact, Sophie can apply six months before her full eligibility date and get day parole."

"Is she a suspect in Sunshine's murder?"

"Although Angelo and Sophie are the prime suspects, all we have is circumstantial evidence at this time. Some of the investigative team think Angelo is the one responsible for killing Sunshine."

"Not me. I know you're probably tired of me saying it, but I still believe Sophie is the primary killer. And I can't believe the justice system is about to set her free. I hope your investigative team uncovers strong evidence against Sophie in Sunshine's murder case."

Stephanie put her hand on my shoulder and said, "Alex, I understand your feelings about Sophie's guilt, but it's all about finding the evidence to criminally charge and convict her in court."

I looked into Stephanie's eyes and said, "You're right. I know I shouldn't get tunnel vision, but it's so frustrating when the police can't get enough evidence to charge and convict someone who's clearly guilty of murder."

Stephanie gave me a hug and told me she understood what I was saying. We walked a little further and then turned around and started walking back toward our cars. On the way back, we chatted about the weather and Corey and Karen and we generally avoided talking anymore about Sophie and Sunshine.

We got back to the cars and we gave each other a hug. "Thanks for meeting me for breakfast and giving me tips about following up at the escort service," she said.

I told her, "If possible, try to keep me in the loop on any new information. I guess I have just as much of a bug about this case as you do."

Stephanie smiled. "I will," she said.

As she was about leave, I gently grabbed her arm and told her, "I'm really happy you decided to make some changes and that you found Corey."

She said, "Alex, I really do appreciate our friendship and your kind thoughts."

I said, "Thanks, and tell Corey I say 'hi' to him."

Then we got into our cars and went our separate ways.

As I drove home, I thought how nice it was to see and spend

time with Stephanie. I was happy she had decided to slow her career down a bit and start enjoying life. Years ago when we'd worked on that joint police service investigation, she told me she had once been married for a short period of time. She never told me specific information as to what had happened in her marriage, but she use to refer to him as 'the jerk' and 'asshole'. They never had children. I guessed from some of her comments that he'd cheated on her. I was glad she'd taken the big step of trusting someone again.

CHAPTER 13

For the next three weeks nothing too exciting happened. Sometimes life is pretty regular. I got up every morning, had coffee with Karen, and kissed her good-bye when she left the house to go to work. Then I went to the gym for a light workout, or sometimes I went for a 45-minute walk. After that, I puttered around the house, sorting through things and trying to downsize the garage, or I dusted off the Plymouth.

I worked the next couple of Sunday night shifts for Allan and I found it a little boring. I hadn't heard from Stephanie for a while, so I spoke to Karen about inviting her and Corey to our house for a barbeque. "That would be great," she said, "But you're not allowed to talk about police stuff all night."

I told Karen, "Maybe just thirty minutes or so, and that will be it."

I phoned Stephanie and she said, "I'm happy to hear your voice. How are you?"

"Good," I said. "How about you?"

She said, "Overall, everything is pretty good. We've been working hard on identifying Sunshine. There have been three different owners of the escort service in five years and the place has a variety of different company names. They employed about 60 part-time girls during the time period we're looking at."

I told her, "It sound like it's going to take a lot of time and resources to track down all those girls and interview them."

"You're not kidding," she said. "But we're making progress, though it's slow going."

I asked Stephanie if she and Corey wanted to come to our place for dinner on Saturday afternoon. "You can sleep over if you want," I said. "That way you guys can let loose a bit."

"Sounds great," said Stephanie. "We're both off work and can come up by around four. I doubt we'll be sleeping over, though. Corey is a light drinker and he will probably drive us home. Plus we have a bunch of things to do on Sunday."

I said, "Great," and gave her our home address.

I was excited that Stephanie and Corey were coming for dinner. I knew Karen would go out of her way preparing a nice dinner and was looking forward to relaxing and having some drinks with my friends.

Karen and I spent a few days cleaning the house and picking up some food and alcoholic beverages. Saturday came and Corey and Stephanie arrived. I greeted them at the door. They brought flowers for Karen and a nice bottle of wine.

We sat around the kitchen island with drinks and munchie snack food, talking as Karen prepared dinner. Stephanie and Corey told me they'd officially moved in together and that they were having some interesting discussions about his out-dated furniture.

Soon, Karen handed me a platter full of steaks and told me it was time to go outside and barbeque. Stephanie offered to help Karen in the kitchen, while Corey and I went outside.

Karen said, "It's no problem, Stephanie. I have everything under control. Now is probably a good time to go outside with the guys and talk cop business. But no more shop talk the rest of the night, okay?"

"No problem," said Stephanie. "I got the message."

I had the barbeque going and was about to throw the steaks on it when Stephanie came outside. She brought Corey and me a couple of beers, and we thanked her. She said, "Karen gave me the big warning. We're having our cop talk now and then after that

I promised there would be no more police talk for the rest of the night." We all laughed.

"I have some good and bad news about the investigation," Stephanie said. "The bad news is that Sophie got early parole and has been released from custody. She's staying at a halfway house on Jarvis Street and has strict parole conditions. A surveillance team has been assigned to periodically watch her."

I just about snorted out my beer as I said, "I can't believe how the justice system works sometimes."

Corey said, "The good news is that we've tracked down a couple of girls who used to work with Sunshine at the escort service. One girl, Melissa Robertson, retired from the prostitution business and moved to Beaver Lake, Ontario. I spoke to Melissa on the phone and she was really upset that Sunshine had been murdered. She was friends with Sunshine, but they hadn't talked to each other for a very long time."

"Did she know her real name?"

"It didn't really sound like it," said Corey. "But she said she had an old cell phone somewhere that might have some texts messages from Sunshine on it. We're sending a couple of investigators up to Beaver Lake to interview her."

I said, "That sounds promising. I hope you guys find something."

"The other girl's street name is Eve, and we're still working on finding out her real name so we can contact her and speak to her," said Corey.

I told them it sounded like that they done some good investigative work and then I said, "I guess that's it for the police talk because the steaks are ready."

We went back inside and had a nice dinner. We chatted about a lot of different things through the evening, but there was no more cop talk. Corey only had one or two drinks, early in the evening, and so by ten o'clock, we were all done and he and Stephanie were ready to leave. We hugged each other goodbye.

"Don't forget to keep me updated on the investigation," I called after them as they drove away.

When they left, Karen commented, "They make a nice couple and seem happy together."

"Yes, I'm glad we invited them for dinner, and I'm happy for them too."

On Sunday night, as I got ready for my last shift as a trash man, I thought about my next bypass surgery, which Dr. Burns had indicated was a good idea to have in the near future. It was tough taking it easy and waiting for him to give the go-ahead. I was taking my heart medication and trying not to stress myself out, but I still didn't feel all that good. I had aches and pains off and on, but I didn't necessarily associate them with my heart. I figured they were probably just caused by old age.

I kissed Karen good night and drove down to Featherstone's to pick up the garbage truck. When I got there, I noticed an envelope under the front windshield wiper. It was from Allan. He said he was selling the truck and he asked me to leave my key in the drop box outside the front door. He told me I'd be driving a brand-new truck that was parked next to his office. He said the truck keys were hidden under the front fender, above the front wheel. I thought, *Allan is lucky no one else opened the letter or he might have had his new truck stolen.* I found the key and got into the cab of the truck. It smelled new, but the used dump box and equipment installed on the rear frame of the truck still stunk of garbage.

I drove over to Pete's and grabbed my coffee, as usual. The hookers were still outside standing around. Some were talking to each other while others were strutting around showing off their goods and trying to pick up customers. As usual, some said, "Hi Alex," or, "Hi, trash man." I said 'hi' back to them.

I sat in the coffee shop for a while, watching customers come and go. I realized I wasn't going to miss this environment too much. Bisson City was now so busy and hectic. I grew up in Bisson City. It used to be a quiet, clean town. At night, everybody was in bed sleeping. Now it seems the city never sleeps. It has really changed.

When I finished my coffee, as usual, I did the cardboard route first and then the garbage route second. After dumping the garbage, I cleaned the box of the truck. There's a small area in the dump yard just for that purpose. Most garbage falls out pretty good when the truck box is hoisted but some gets stuck in there. If you move the truck and brake suddenly, it jilts the box and causes the remaining garbage to fall out, and then you wash out the box with a high-pressure hose.

Once I'd done all that, I drove back to the city core. I'd finished my run an hour early and was toying with the idea of parking the truck and going home early, but at the last minute, I decided to try to find Joe and say good-bye to him, since I only had one more shift left. Once I quit this job, I didn't think I would have much chance to come downtown to see him.

I drove around to a few locations where I'd seen him in the past. He move around a lot and so I spent nearly 30 minutes looking for him, with no success. Then I decided to drive down to the waterfront warehouse where he'd witnessed Sophie and Angelo dumping the last murdered girl's body into the water. I knew he liked to camp by the railroad steam pipe, so I thought he might be there.

I pulled up to the isolated, old warehouse area. There wasn't much for light down there, but I could see a few box cars and tankers on the train tracks and I could also see the steam pipe running adjacent to the train tracks about two feet off the ground. I drove toward the area slowly, trying to spot Joe's shopping cart. Things were pretty quiet until, when I rounded the corner of one of the buildings, in the distance I could see a figure moving erratically on the tracks.

It was just after 4:30 a.m. and I wondered, *is that Joe?* As I got closer, it seemed that the figure was swinging something. I wasn't sure what was going on but I felt anxious. Something didn't seem right. Suddenly I saw Joe's shopping cart, with all the plastic bags tied to it. It was off to the side, near the person who was dancing around.

The person didn't stop what they were doing despite the fact that I was getting closer to them. This new truck of Allen's was much quieter than the old one, but it was still a big diesel truck. I thought, *that person must be very focused on what they're doing if they haven't noticed me driving toward them.*

As I got closer, my headlights shone on the figure and I realized, *that's not Joe … this guy has shorter hair, a heavier build and no beard.* Now I could see the person was moving so erratically because he was frantically swinging a pole or a shovel or something at a lump on the ground. I was about 30 feet away now, driving slowly towards the action as I tried to figure out what the hell was going on. Just then, the person raised her head and looked right at me and I clearly recognized Sophie. *What the hell? Is Sophie hitting Joe with a shovel?*

Thoughts ran through my head at warp speed. I started to panic. I had to get close real fast and help Joe. I stepped on the gas pedal and the brand-new truck sped up a lot more than I thought it would. There was only about fifteen feet between us now, but she didn't run. Instead, she stepped back to swing the shovel again and so I clipped her hard with the corner of the truck. As I slammed on the brakes, she went flying through the air.

I quickly got out of the truck. I glanced at Sophie. She was not moving. Then I went over to see how Joe was. He was on his back and had been badly beaten up. He had a bloody face and deep, open wounds on his head probably from the edges of the shovel. I bent down, pushed his hair away from his face, grabbed his wrist and tried to find a pulse. I checked a couple of times, with no results. He was unconscious, not breathing and had blood coming from his ear. I checked his head and I felt something unusual and sticky—brain matter coming from the side of his head. He was dead.

Then I went over to check on Sophie. She had an obvious deformity to her neck, and her head was positioned in a very unusual way. I checked for a pulse but could not find one. I believed she had a broken neck. She was also clearly dead.

Immediately, I got out my cell phone and called the police … and that's when the most incredible pain shot up my arm and across my chest. I heard someone speaking on the phone, but I couldn't talk. I wasn't able to stand, so I dropped down to my knees. I was able to say, "Send help," before I fell flat onto the ground.

As I lay on the ground, I started silently panicking. *I just killed someone and now I'm about to die,* I thought. I groped around for my cell phone but couldn't find it in the darkness. I struggled to get up and finally, after a couple of minutes, I was able to awkwardly stand. I was able to limp back to my truck, but it was slow going and I was clutching my chest and massaging my heart the whole way.

I got into the truck and found my medication. I dumped a pile of pills into my mouth. Some of the pills missed and fell out the truck's window onto the ground, but I didn't care. I sat there sweating and holding my chest, hoping the police could ping my phone and get here right away. I was in an isolated, dark area behind a large building and I was concerned that police and ambulance wouldn't be able to find me. Sick and in pain as I was, I decided to drive the trash truck up to the street so they'd see me and then I could direct them to Joe and Sophie.

I don't know how I managed to do it, but I made it to the street only to find that no one was there. I was confused and I didn't know what to do. The pain in my chest was constant and I wasn't sure if the medication had helped or not. Then I thought, *I'm not going to die in a garbage truck in downtown Bisson.* If this was it, at least I wanted to die in my own pickup truck.

When I'd dropped my phone, the line had still been open with the police dispatcher. *The police should be able to find my phone. But where are they? If I wait much longer I might die.* I decided to leave. I couldn't stay. I was certain the police would find the murder scene and quickly figure out who I was, and what my connection to the dead people was. But I had to go.

I could hardly see and I could hardly drive. I had a lot of trouble seeing the street lights; they were very blurry. I drove with one hand on the wheel and the other on my chest, and I had a lot of trouble making turns. The steering wheel was large and the turning radius for the truck was wide. Somehow, though, I made it back to Allan's yard and slid out of the truck. From there, I was able to get into my pickup truck and start it. Then I sat for a moment trying to figure out what I should do. Should I go to the hospital? Should I wait for the police? I was panicking and my brain wasn't working right. All I wanted to do was go home. I didn't want to die in the hospital; I wanted to die in my house.

I started driving up the highway towards home. Northbound traffic was light, but southbound traffic was heavy. I could hardly see as headlights going into town kept flashing in my eyes, almost blinding me. I drove hunched over with only one eye open.

About half-way home the constant pain across my chest forced me to pull over onto the shoulder of the highway and park. I immediately poured the rest of my medication into my mouth and then I must have passed out. I woke up a while later and didn't know where I was at first. Then I realized I was still in my pickup, parked on the side of the highway. I glanced at the clock. An hour and a half had passed and it was nearly seven-thirty in the morning. Southbound highway traffic was now bumper to bumper and hardly moving. Northbound traffic was also a lot heavier.

I still had some pain in my chest, but it wasn't as bad as before. However, I was sweating and confused and didn't remember why I had stopped on the shoulder of the highway. My vision was blurry and I had to squint out of one eye to see. Slowly, I remembered having the heart attack. Then I remembered poor Joe, and that

Sophie had killed him and I had tried to stop her. *I killed Sophie with the garbage truck.*

I knew now that I had been right about Sophie being the mastermind behind the murders. She was a psychopath and she had killed Joe to get even with him for being the eyewitness that got her and Angelo arrested. She knew he lived in the waterfront warehouse area; she'd probably seen him on television just as I had.

However, I wasn't sure if hitting Sophie with the truck was the right thing to do. I knew I could use reasonable force to stop a murderer, but was hitting someone with a garbage truck justified? *At least she won't be around to kill anyone else,* I thought.

I was still in a great deal of pain and confused about what to do. I started to drive up the highway again, sticking to the slow traffic lane and steering with my right hand as my left side seemed partially paralyzed. I was careful, as I didn't want to cause an accident. A few people beeped at me to go faster, but I ignored them.

It was now about eight-thirty in the morning. All I could think about was getting home and just laying down for a while. If I died, I wanted to do it there. If I lived, I hoped the excruciating pain would pass and knew it probably wouldn't take the police long to find me.

When I arrived home, I was able only to get in the front door before I fell onto the floor. Karen had already gone to work and so I just lay on the hallway tiles for a while. They were nice and cool.

I heard the house phone ring a couple of times but there was no way I could get up to answer it, so it went to voicemail. I just couldn't seem to get up, or even to move.

It's funny what you think about when you're dying. I thought about Karen and the kids, and that I should call an ambulance. I wondered if Stephanie was going to arrest me for killing Sophie. I also thought I couldn't survive being in prison.

As I lay there, slowly a little bit of strength returned and after a couple of hours, I was finally able to slowly crawl my way into a standing position. I went into the kitchen to get a drink of water. My chest felt stiff and I was a little disoriented. I found the aspirin container and I took some aspirin.

As I stood there gulping aspirin, I looked into the living room and there, on the mantel over the fireplace, I saw the urn with Kobe's ashes in it. I thought, *if I die, Kobe's ashes will still be on the mantel.* Karen and I had discussed spreading his ashes along the ravine route that we use to walk him through, but we never seemed to have the time to do it. For some strange reason, it was really important to me to do it now. I didn't know how long I was going to be around and I was going to take him for one last walk. I was ready to spread Kobe's ashes along the ravine trail.

I wrote a quick note to Karen and left it on the kitchen counter. I told her in the note that I loved her and the kids very much, that I was sorry for killing Sophie with the garbage truck and that I was just trying to save my friend Joe. I told her to look in the top drawer of our bedroom dresser where I had stored all our financial stuff, plus letters for her and the kids.

Then I thought, *if only if Karen knew what was going on. Maybe I should phone her.* The pain was getting steadily stronger in my left arm, and the pressure on my chest was constant. Thoughts raced through my mind as to what I should do. I was very confused and disoriented. I had mixed feelings about whether I should call an ambulance or not. I was pretty sure this was more than a mini-heart attack. I was pretty sure I was going to die, no matter what I did.

Should I call Stephanie and explain what happened to Sophie? Did I do enough for Old Joe? Was I thinking straight when I left the scene? I was sure Sophie killed Joe intentionally. But did I kill Sophie intentionally? *Did I have enough time to stop the truck, jump out and stop her from hitting Joe?*

I wondered why I left the scene and drove all the way home. *That was crazy,* I told myself. I guess I just wanted to die at home in my own bed. I had lived in that home for 30 years. I wanted to die in it too.

I knew Stephanie and Corey were smart investigators and it would only be only a matter of time before Stephanie figured out that I had hit Sophie Martino with the garbage truck. The evidence was all there: the emergency phone call I had made, the damage to the truck and my cell phone at the scene. There were probably truck skid marks near Sophie's body to boot.

Whatever. Suddenly, I didn't care. I grabbed Kobe's ashes from the mantle. It was time for us to have one last walk together. I decided to remove his ashes from the heavy urn and put them in a plastic bag so I could carry them in my pocket. I went into the garage and used a hammer to break open the urn and then I carefully poured the ashes into the plastic bag. By now, I was sweating so much I had to keep wiping my forehead and the pain in my left arm and chest area was constant. I grabbed more medication and took it, but this time the pain wasn't stopping. *Fuck you, pain,* I thought. I went to the liquor cabinet, found some whiskey and had a big drink.

I left the house and started walking slowly down the street. The pain increased in my chest, arm, back and legs, but all I could think was, *Kobe, old boy, we're going on our last walk together.* I limped along, trying not to fall, for about ten minutes. I was determined. I had to keep going; I had to go past the duck pond and get to the ravine trail.

As I rounded the corner, I saw an unmarked police car coming in my direction. It looked Stephanie and Corey had found me. The car stopped next to me. It was them. They got out and came over to me. Stephanie, clearly worried, said in a rush, "Alex, what the fuck happened? What's going on? We found your cell phone. How come you didn't stay at the scene?" Then she looked more closely at me and said, "You look terrible. Are you okay? Should I call an ambulance?"

"I'm not feeling that good," I told her, "But I'm okay. I was working my last shift last night and I went looking for Joe to say good bye to him. I found him near the rear of the warehouse and I saw Sophie hitting him with a shovel. I had to stop her, so I hit her with the truck. I was calling the police for help and then I had a heart attack. I thought I was dying and for some reason it seemed like a good idea to get home and die there," I admitted.

"Geez, Alex," said Stephanie, her eyes wide. Then she said that Joe had been rushed to the hospital, but was still alive.

Corey said, "Sophie didn't make it though. She died at the scene. And Alex? I think we should call an ambulance for you."

I told him, "No, please don't, I'm starting to feel better."

Corey said, "Then we have to talk to you about what happened, which means we have to take you downtown to the police station to sort this out."

Stephanie said. "You know the formalities have to be dealt with. We have to do a thorough investigation. We have to interview you." Then she asked again, "Are you sure you're okay? You don't look very good."

I lied to them and downplayed how I was actually feeling. "My chest is sore, that's all," I told them. "I'm prepared to give you a full statement downtown. But can you give me a half-hour? I need to do something first."

Corey asked, "What you want to do?"

I started to tear up as I explained that I was carrying my dog's ashes in my pocket. I told them, "Just let me spread his ashes in the pond and along the ravine trail, and then I will go with you. I can't really run away. I have no steam left. You can watch me walk if you want. There are no trees to block the view. You can meet me at the end of the path. I promise, after I say good bye to Kobe, I'll cooperate fully with the investigation. Please let me do this."

I stood there sweating and out of breath, thinking, *they can't possibly know how much pain I'm in.*

Stephanie looked puzzled, "Alex, I'm confused," she said. "Do you really think I expect you to run away? Why would I think that?" I saw her exchange a look with Corey, and then she said soothingly, "Sure, Alex. We'll watch you from a distance and meet you at the end of the ravine trail."

I said, "Okay, and thank you."

I thought, *perhaps Stephanie is catching on how sick I am ...* I started walking slowly towards the pond. The pain was increasing but I wanted to do this. For eight years Karen and I had taken Kobe for runs and walks on this route. I stopped on the bridge near the edge of the pond. Karen, Kobe and I use to stop here to feed the geese and ducks pieces of bread. Usually, it was one piece for the birds and another for Kobe.

As I threw a handful of his ashes into the water, I said, "Kobe, old boy, maybe I'll see you soon." Then I walked further into the ravine as Stephanie and Corey waited for me, off in the distance, in their police car.

I was hardly walking now. The pain was so bad I could barely see. My vision was blurring, so I stopped to catch my breath. I took out the plastic bag full of Kobe's ashes and decided it would be easier to just spread them along the trail as I walked. As I sprinkled his ashes I talked to Kobe. "Those were good days, right Kobe?" I asked, as if he was actually standing right next to me.

Finally, I couldn't walk anymore and so I stopped. I was having trouble keeping my balance. I felt guilty about what I'd done. *Was hitting Sophie with the truck my only option?* She was trying to kill Joe. Did I have any other option? I wondered if God was punishing me and killing me for killing her.

For 30 years I had been an honest, hard-working cop. I believed in the justice system and in honesty and truth. But in this *specific* investigation, clearly the justice system had failed. It freed a serial killer to kill again. There was no doubt in my mind that Sophie Martino had killed all those girls, including Sunshine. But she'd been released from custody *way* too early, playing the 'poor victim' card and winning the game. I knew she'd reoffend—but

I didn't expect her to hunt down and try to kill my friend Joe. *I stopped her,* I thought. *I did what I had to do, Kobe.*

I struggled to walk further, took a few steps and stopped. I just couldn't walk anymore. I fell to the ground onto one knee. In the distance, I saw Stephanie and Corey jump out of their car and start running toward me. I heard Stephanie screaming, "Alex, Alex, Alex!" and I saw Corey yelling into his cell phone.

I fell flat on the ground on my stomach. I was able to lift my head a bit and I looked toward Stephanie and said, "I'm sorry, I'm sorry." As my eyes closed, I saw Kobe standing there next to me, his tongue was hanging out and his tail was wagging.

I said, "Kobe, I'm coming to play with you."

AUTOBIOGRAPHY

Norm Meech is a first-time author and a full-time police officer who has spent over 40 years with three different police agencies in the province of Ontario, Canada. During his career, Norm spent more than 14 years working on criminal investigations.

Although this is a fictional novel, Norm wanted to write about what it is like to conduct a homicide investigation, and to show how police officers are affected by tragedies as much as civilians are. Police see the worst part of society at much closer range than most people, which puts them at risk for elevated instances of substance abuse and post-traumatic stress disorder. In this book, Norm wanted to expose why this is so, and to underline the drive and determination police officers have despite the sometimes-crushing demands of the job.

Norm believes that one of the greatest honours a police officer can have is to be responsible for investigating the death of another human being, and to bring closure to the families of the victims of homicide and other violent crimes.

Norm Meech's Personal History

Norm graduated from Oakwood Collegiate High School in Toronto, Ontario in June 1976. In October 1976, at the age of 18 years, Norm was hired by the Metropolitan Toronto Police Service as a police cadet. He was assigned to the Summons Bureau, serving summons and subpoenas in various divisions throughout the City of Toronto. Unsure about a policing career, Norm resigned from the Metropolitan Toronto Police in September 1978.

On December 3, 1979, Norm was hired as a police constable by the Canadian National Police Service. He performed a variety of policing duties in uniform and worked in criminal investigations for nearly eight years.

On June 9, 1997, the Barrie Police Service hired Norm and he remains there to this day, holding the rank of staff sergeant.

Norm began his career in Barrie in the uniformed patrol division, but on November 1, 2000, he was transferred to the Criminal Investigations Division, General Assignments Unit. While working as a detective constable, he was responsible investigation of a variety of criminal matters.

On December 1, 2001 Norm was promoted to the rank of sergeant. He became the supervisor in charge of the Sexual Assault/Domestic Violence Unit until April 1, 2005.

On April 4, 2005, Norm became the supervisor in charge of the Major Crime Unit. The Major Crime Unit works on serious crimes, such as homicide investigations. Norm was the case manager for a number of homicide investigations.

On April 6, 2009, Norm was promoted to the rank of staff sergeant and transferred to the Operations Services Division. He was a platoon staff sergeant for two different platoons.

On April 4, 2011, he was transferred to the position of detective sergeant, in the Investigative Services Division. One of the units he supervised was the Homicide Unit.

On January 5, 2014, Norm became the detective sergeant of the Specialized Investigations Division, supervising the Homicide, Forensic Identification, and Technological Crime Units.

On September 25, 2017, Norm was transferred to the Professional Standards Unit, Executive Services Division, where he is currently employed.

While employed by the Barrie Police Service, Norm has also

had the opportunity to be a crisis negotiator as well as a member the Public Order Team and the Containment Team.

Norm is a proud member of the Barrie Police Service and is grateful to have had the opportunity to work for the City of Barrie for the past 22 years.

On May 8, 2019, the Barrie Police Service presented Norm with his 40-year exemplary police service bar.

Norm is especially proud to have had the opportunity to work in, and supervise, the Barrie Police Service Homicide Unit.

Norm would like to recognize and acknowledge his wife Monica and their two children, Hunter and Haleigh, who have supported him in his career for the past 25 years.

CPSIA information can be obtained
at www.ICGtesting.com
Printed in the USA
LVHW031910291019
635758LV00003B/3/P

9 780228 816188